George Ade

Artie

A Story of the Streets and Town

George Ade

Artie
A Story of the Streets and Town

ISBN/EAN: 9783337400286

Printed in Europe, USA, Canada, Australia, Japan

Cover: Foto ©Andreas Hilbeck / pixelio.de

More available books at **www.hansebooks.com**

ARTIE

A Story of the Streets and Town

BY

GEORGE ADE

PICTURES BY

JOHN T. McCUTCHEON

CHICAGO

HERBERT S. STONE & CO.

1896

ARTIE

I

One day Mrs. Morton, wife of the city manager, came to the offices and in polite brigandage compelled each man in the room to pay fifty cents for a ticket to the charity entertainment. This entertainment was to be given at a South Side church on the following Wednesday evening. Artie bought a ticket with apparent willingness.

" I do n't want you young men to think that I 'm robbing you of this money," said Mrs. Morton. " I want you to come to the entertainment. You 'll enjoy it, really."

" Blanchard can go all right," suggested Miller, with a wink at young Mr. Hall. "He lives within a few blocks of your church."

"Then he must come," said Mrs. Morton decisively. "Won't you, Mr. Blanchard ? "

"Sure," replied Artie, blushing deeply.

"Why, Mrs. Morton, he has n't been in a church for three years," said Miller.

"I do n't believe it," and she turned to Artie, who was shaking his fist at Miller. "Now, Mr. Blanchard, I want you to promise me faithfully that you 'll come."

"I 'll be there all right," said he, smiling feebly.

"Remember, you 've promised," and as she went out she shook her finger at him as a final reminder.

"Well, are you going ? " asked Miller.

Artie put on his lofty manner and gazed at his office companions with seeming cold- ness.

"What 's it to you whether I do or not ? Did n't you hear what I said to her ? Sure I 'm goin'. I 've got as much right to go out and do the heavy as any o' you pin-heads. If I like their show I'll help 'em out next time — get a couple o' handy boys and put on a six-round go for a finish. Them people never saw anything good."

"I'll bet you do n't go," spoke up young Mr. Hall.

Artie laughed dryly. "You guys must think I'm a quitter, to be scared out by any little old church show," said he.

That was the last said of the charity entertainment until Thursday morning, when Artie, after dusting off his desk, strolled up to Miller and gave him a friendly blow, known to ringside patrons as a "kidney-punch."

"Ouch!" exclaimed Miller.

"Well, I goes," said Artie.

"Where?" asked Miller, who had forgotten.

"Where? Well, that's a good thing. To the church show — the charity graft. I did n't do a thing but push my face in there about eight o'clock last night, and I was 'it' from the start. Say, I like that church, and if they 'll put in a punchin'-bag and a plunge they can have my game, I 'll tell you those."

"Did you see Mrs. Morton?"

"How's that, boy? Did I see her? Say, she treated me out o' sight. She meets me at the door, puts out the glad hand and says: 'Hang up your lid and come into the game.'"

"I never heard her talk like that," suggested Miller.

"Well, that 's what she meant. She 's all right, too, and the only wonder to me is how she ever happened to tie herself up to that slob. It 's like hitchin' up a four-time winner 'longside of a pelter. He ain't in her class, not for a minute or a part of a minute. What kills me off is how all these dubs make their star winnin's. W'y, out there last night I see the measliest lot o' jays — regular Charley-boys — floatin' around with queens. I

4

wish somebody 'd tell me how they cop 'em out. Do n't it kill you dead to see a swell girl — you know, a regular peach — holdin' on to some freak with side whiskers and thinkin' she 's got a good thing? That 's right. She thinks he 's all right. Anyway, she acts the part. And say, you know Percival, that works over in the bank — little Percy, the perfect lady. There 's a guy I 've known for five years, and so help me, if he gets on a street-car where I am, I get off and walk. That ain't no lie. I pass him up. I say, ' You 're all right, Percy, and you can take the car to yourself,' and then I duck."

" Was he there ?"

" The whole thing ! That ain't no kid. He was the real papa — the hit o' the piece. One on each arm, see ? — and puttin' up the large, juicy con talk. They was beauts too ; you could n't beat 'em, not in a thousand years. There they was, holdin' to this wart. Up goes my hands

in the air, and I says to myself: ' Percy,
you 're all right. I would n't live on the
same street with you, but you 're all right
at that.' But he could n't see me."

" Could n't see you ? "

" No, he lost his eyesight. He looked
at me, but he was too busy to see me.
No, he had on his saucy coat and that
touch-me-not necktie, and oh, he was
busy. He was n't doin' a thing. I think
I 'll give the bank a line on Percy. Any
man that wears that kind of a necktie
had n't ought to handle money. But you
ought to seen the two he had. I'd like to
know how he does it. I had a notion to
go up to one o' the girls and say: 'What's
the matter ? Ain't you ever seen any
others ? ' "

" Did you like the show ? " asked Miller.

" It 's this way. They liked it, and so "
— with a wave of the hand — " let 'em
have it. If they put the same turns on at
any variety house the people 'd tear down

the buildin', tryin' to get their coin back.
Mrs. Morton got me a good seat and then
backcapped the show a little before it
opened up, so I did n't expect to be pulled
out o' my chair — and I was n't. If I'd
been near the door I 'd 'a' sneaked early
in the game, but, like a farmer, I let her
put me way up in front. I saw I was up
against it, so I lasted the best way I could.
Two or three o' the songs was purty fair,
but the woman that trifled with the piano
for about a half an hour was very much on
the bummy bum. Then there was a guy
called an entertainer, that told some o' the
gags I used to hear when my brother
took me to the old Academy and held me
on his lap. But he got 'em goin', just the
same. 'Well,' I says to myself, 'what'd
a couple o' hot knockabouts do to this
push ?' On the dead, I do n't believe any
o' them people out there ever saw a good
show. It just goes to prove that there's
lots of people with stuff that think they

know what 's goin' on in town, but they
do n't.   I ain't got no kick comin', only it
was a yellow show, and I 'm waitin' for
forty-five cents change."

"I should think you would have got
the worth of your money simply by seeing
so many good-looking girls," said Miller.

"The girls are all right, only I think
they 're a little slow on pickin' the right
kind.   If I had time I 'd go over to that
church and make a lot o' them Reubs look
like thirty-cent pieces.   Not that I 'm
strong on the con talk, but I know I 'd be
in it with them fellows.   I think it must
be a case of nerve.   That 's all there is
to 'em — is nerve.   But the girls —
wow ! "

" Beauties, eh ? "

" Lollypaloozers ! "

: CAUTIOUS BOY

II

"It's hard goin' this morning," remarked Artie, as he performed the difficult feat of removing his rubbers without touching his hands to them, "and I ain't much of a mud-horse." He telescoped his cuffs and put them on a hook, yawned lazily and said : "I've got a peach of a head."

"Were you out?" asked Miller.

"Naw, I was settin' in an easy game o' poker. None of us stood to win car fare, but I went in, thinkin' I might get 'em loosened up and pull out the price of a Christmas present for the girl."

"Did you?"

"Well, I should say nit. I think I'll have to duck on that present or else go out with a stockin' full o' sand. You never see such a sure-thing crowd in your life."

9

" Where were you playing ? "

" Over at Kennedy's room. He got me to come over and had a couple of his friends there. Oh, but they was hot members! One of 'em whenever he got better 'n jacks up, always lost his voice and could n't keep count o' the chips. Then he 'd stop the game every three minutes to see how he stood with himself. He 'd stack up, you know, an' feel in his pockets and then he 'd say : ' I 'm forty-seven cents loser.' He was the best I ever see."

" Were you playing for money ? " asked young Mr. Hall.

" Playin' for —— now, would n't that upper-cut you ? Sure. You did n't think this was a game o' muggins, like you boys play up at your little old cycle club? This was the real old army game. I guess I saw as much as two bones change hands."

" How did you come out ? " asked Miller.

"Wait and I'll tell you. We kind o' petered along there for two or three hours or so, makin' two call five and as high as fifteen cents to see, everybody keepin' books and beefin' about the way the hands was runnin' and showin' up the cards when nobody come in, and tellin' what they might a' done if they'd done purty well, an' so on — real gambler talk — till I says to myself, 'I'll try it, an' if it do n't go, it's a baby risk.' I gets a pair of type-writers and stays in. All of 'em playin', see? Kennedy leads off. I think he tossed in seven white chips; anyway, he was strong. Then this boy that was keepin' tab on his stack all the time, he had to think it all over and have another talk with himself and skin his cards three or four times, and then he put in. Up to me — see? I kind o' gives the gentle push to half a samoleon and says: 'Comrades, it'll cost you fifty c. apiece to linger in my society.' Say, you never see people so busy. Kennedy has a long talk with himself and counts his stuff, and then he says to this safe player at the right o' me : 'Are you goin' to call him?' 'Nix,' I says. 'This ain't tennis; this is poker.' Kennedy looked a few spots off his hand, and then he says : 'Well, I'm out,' just as if he said : 'Well, I lose eight thousand on wheat to-day.'"

" Did the other fellow stay?" asked Miller.

" Stay nothin'! He had the heart failure when he see that half. I pulled in the dough and picked up the cards. 'What did you have?' says Kennedy. 'Oh,' I says, 'I did n't have nothin' but five nines.' 'No,' he says, 'on the square, what *did* you have?' I told him it was against the rules for me to say, but it was a cinch I had him done. 'Well,' he says, 'I had three kings.' That ain't no kid, neither. The geezer was settin' there lookin' into three kings all the time."

" Why, he had you beat, did n't he ? "
exclaimed young Mr. Hall.

" Not in a thousand years. Did n 't I
tell you I got the stuff — quite a bundle
o' money, too. I think there was thirty-
six cents. Talk about your Monte Carlo
boys ! Them guys last night was the gam-
iest I ever set down with."

" Well, now, did n't you have to tell
him what you had ? " inquired young Mr.
Hall.

" Not accordin' to the league rules for
this year. Did I have to tell ? You 're
all right, boy."

" How did you come out ? " persisted
Miller.

"W'y, what chance did I have to get into
'em ? Talk about safe playin'! They're
like the stock-yards man that wanted to
fight Sullivan. ' I 'll fight him,' he says,
' if you blindfold Sullivan and gi' me an
ax.' That was the way with them dubs.
They liked the color o' my money, but

ARTIE

they would n't take no risk. After that
first saucy crack with the half I laid low
three or four hands, and then I knocked
'em a horrible twister. It was a jack pot,
and this cautious boy at the right o' me
opened it. I stay, see? Why should n't
I, when I had two, four, six, seven and
nine, in three different colors, all in my
mit? I stands pat on the draw, and then
the first crack out o' the box I whoops it
a half — fifty kopecks. What does he do?
He could n't drop his hand too quick. Another case o' licked in a punch. He shows
jacks up for openers and then starts to pick
up my hand, but I stood him off. I says:
'Nay, nay, Pauline, there 's some things
so good that it costs money to see 'em.'
I told him that when he wanted to get wise
to what was in my hand all he had to do
was to dig up his bit and come in. 'Well,'
he says, 'I don't want to lose my stuff.'
On the level, no kiddin', that 's what he
said — that he did n't want to lose his

stuff. I told him he was in the wrong kind of a game — that he ought to be playin', 'Heavy, heavy, hangs over your head.'"

"You have n't told us yet how you came out," said young Mr. Hall.

"Well, I kept on layin' low, and then every fourth hand or so comin' in with a half-dollar and takin' the pot. Finally, after I 'd sprung it on 'em about a dozen times and was gettin' quite a stack in front o' me, I stood pat on a hand and tried 'em again. 'Hold on,' says this cautious boy, shakin' all over, 'hold on, don't take that!' I told him I would n't take it till it come time. Then him and Kennedy had a long spiel to themselves. Kennedy was out, of course, not bein' able to show up better 'n threes. He advised the boy to see me. Both of 'em looked at the hand and sized me up, and finally this boy that was holdin' the hand said he 'd go halves with Kennedy and make me spread what I had. They had some more of the talk and at last they put in a quarter apiece. 'I ain't got a thing but a flush,' I says, and I lays down four hearts and a diamond."

" That was n't a ——," began young Mr. Hall.

" Sh!" said Miller.

" You ought 'o heard the roar," resumed Artie, giving young Mr. Hall a reproving glance. "Kennedy hollered the worst of all. 'That ain't no flush,' he says. 'Of course it is,' I come back; 'ain't they all one color?' With that they both begin talkin' at once, showin' me how it was a flush had to be all hearts or all diamonds and that sort o' business. I waited till they got through, and then I said I was dead sore about not bein' next to the point. I says to 'em: 'I been playin' them hands for flushes all night.' The old gag, see? They never tumbled, though. You never heard such kickin'. Them guys thought I'd been playin' red and

black hands all the time. This cautious
boy figured he could 'a' won four bucks
if he 'd called me every time I stood pat.
Say, you 'd died if you 'd heard him."

" Well, who won the pot?" asked
Miller.

" I think you 're about as bright on the
game as they was. W'y, that chump had
a full house, nines on somethin'. Soon
as he took the half I said I 'd stop —
would n't play no more till I learned to
read the hands. We all cashed in, and
what do you think? I was seventy-three
cents to the good. There I set like a big
stiff for five hours and pulled against them
marks for seventy-three cents. Kennedy
lose fifty-four cents, an' I 'll make a guess
right now he ain't through kickin' yet."

III

While they were at lunch a square envelope of a delicate pink color was placed
on Artie's table.

It was addressed in very blue ink to
" Mr. Arthur Blanchard, Esq."

Furthermore, the stamp was placed up-
side down on the upper left-hand corner of
the envelope. According to the code of
the " stamp flirtation" this means either,
" Write soon" or " I am longing to see
you."

When the recipient is certain as to the
feelings of the one who has written, he or
she may take this unusual position of the
stamp to mean even more than is written
in the code.

There may be some ignorant persons
who do not know that when a lady passes

a handkerchief across her face this is a signal to the gentleman friend, standing in front of the cigar store, that she must speak with him soon.

Again, when a gentleman carries his umbrella grasped by the middle with the handle pointing backward he is making a declaration of love to all women whom he encounters. He may be utterly unconscious of the fact, but any one who understands the leading signals of the "umbrella flirtation" will know what is meant when a gentleman deliberately holds his umbrella in that position.

Furthermore, if he carried his umbrella handle forward and inclined at forty-five degrees it would mean " We must part."

A study of that interesting yellow volume wherein are set down all the secrets of flirtation by means of fan, handkerchief, glove, umbrella, walking-stick, postage stamp, book, etc., etc., will show that a deep significance attaches to the most ordinary procedures. Even the hoisting of an umbrella or the mopping of a damp brow may be construed as an expression of hatred, or the very reverse.

If a young man is too bashful or too diplomatic to make a frank declaration of love all he has to do is to " crumple the dance programme in his left hand," and the young woman who has studied the yellow volume will know that he means " I cannot live without you." (See " programme flirtations.")

Artie no sooner saw the envelope than he smiled broadly. He knew the meaning of the upside-down stamp, but Miller did not.

"Oh, well, I guess I ain't strong on the North Side," said Artie, as he held the envelope up to the light. " She writes a swell letter, don't she? You might think, to size it up, it come from the Lake Shore Drive. She's a little queer on the spellin', but her heart's in the right place."

ARTIE

" Is that from one of your lady friends? "
asked young Mr. Hall, with a side wink
at Miller. Since Hall had been attending the whist parties he had shown a
disposition to be quietly scornful of Artie's social connections.

"Never you mind," replied Artie. "This
ain't for boys."

He opened the letter and read it carefully, occasionally remarking: "I ain't a
bit strong here."

" Are we going to hear it?" asked Miller, who was biting his pencil with curi-
osity.

" Not in a thousand. What do you
take me for? This letter's for me and
I'm the only boy that gets 'em, too, I'll
tell you those."

" That's what she says, I suppose."

" Is that so? I come purt' near knowin'
how strong I am with her. There ain't
nobody else one-two-seven. They ain't
even in the ' also rans.' "

"Well, you must be solid."

"Solid? W'y, I'm one o' the family. You could n't queer me with that girl. I've made the play at the old folks, on the square. The old man's dead with me. I went to see her one night and she was out, so I had to set there for about an hour and pipe him the best I could. Le 'me tell you."

Then Artie had to stop and laugh.

"I never put you next to how I come to meet her, did I? Say, there was the funniest thing ever. It must 'a. been three months ago, a fellow holds me up for the price of a ticket to a dance up on North Clark street. I did n't expect to break in, but when the night come there was nothin' else in sight so I hot-foots up to the dance. It was a sucker play, too, because I might 'a' known it 'd be a case of takin' the horse cars to get back to the West Side. I had some new togs, a new pair o' patent leathers and — well, I don't like to star

ARTIE

myself, but I guess I was about as good
as the best. And this crowd up there was
purty-y-y punk; very much on the hand-
me-down order."

" It was n't a full dress affair, then ? "
asked Miller, laughing.

" Oh me, oh my! Full dress? W'y, if a
guy 'd floated in there with one o' them
Clarence outfits they 'd 'a' hung him across
a chandelier. Some o' them was dead
tough and the others was hams. It was
frosty, too. I could n 't see any folks I
knew, so I stood around there on one foot
kind o' rubber-neckin' to find an openin'.
Finally I see Mamie over in one corner."

" So that 's her name, is it — Mamie ?"

" I guess you got past my guard that
time. Yes, that 's her name, Mamie. As
soon as I see her — everything else off. It
was a sure enough case of ' only one girl.'
' In a minute,' I says, and I swore I 'd
get next no matter what kind of a brash
play I had to make. Say, she 's a dream.

23

That's right. If she had the clothes she'd make the best of 'em look foolish."

"I believe you're stuck on her," ventured Miller.

" Mebbe that ain't no lie neither. She'd make anybody daffy. As I was sayin', she was settin' over in the corner, and I could see that a Johnny-on-the-spot, with a big badge, marked 'Committee,' was tryin' to keep cases on her. He waltzed with her once or twice, but most o' the time he had to be out on the floor yellin' 'Two more couples wanted,' and all that business. He was makin' himself the whole thing. Well, I got friendly with a guy that was standin' around, the same as myself, tryin' to break in, an' I says to him: 'I want you to do me a favor. Take me over and gi' me a knock-down to the queen in the corner.' He said he didn't know her. 'What's the diff?' I says. 'Ain't you got your nerve with you?' Well, he was all right.

He took me over and says : 'Miss Lum-yum and-so-and-so,' fakin' it as he went, 'I want you to shake hands with my friend, Mr. Ta-ra-m-m-m,' and then he ducked."

"What was it he called you?"

"He did n't call me nothin'. He just made a bluff. She says to me, 'I did n't ketch the name.' 'Livingstone,' I says, 'Herbert Livingstone. I'm on the board o' trade.' That board o' trade business has been done to death, but I guess it went with her. I asked her for her name and she give it to me — straight. 'How about the next dance?' I says. She said it was all right if Mr. Wilson did n't come around and claim it. I asked her if the boy with the badge owned her and she laughed. I see that he did n't have no cinch on it, so I just started in. I put up the tall talk, jollied her along, danced with her three times — well, of course, you could n't blame her. I sprung them

West Side manners o' mine on her and
I had her won. Finally his rabs with
the banner on his coat comes around and
begins to roast her. Sore? You never
see a man so sore."

" Why did n't you stop him ? "

"Oh, I did n't stop him, did I ? Mebbe
I let him go right ahead and have his own
way. You ought o' seen me. I put up
a bluff that 'd curl your hair. I went up
to him and I breathed it right in his ear.
I leaned against him. ' Look here,' I says,
' you screw right away from here. We
do n't like your style. If you open your
face to this lady again to-night I 'll separate
you from your breath.' Did he go? Well,
I should say yes. He did n't want none o'
my game."

" Did n't she get mad? " asked young
Mr. Hall, who had become intensely interested.

" What, after he 'd weakened that way?
His name was pants, then and there. I

says to her: ' That fellow 's got a horrible
rind to think he can set on the same side
o' the room with you.' Then she said
she did n't know what she 'd do, because
he 'd brought her there and her pa-pah
would be crazy if she went runnin' around
the street by her lonelies. You see, I
was n't doin' all the stringin'. She kept
playin' that 'pa-pah' gag on me. Pa-pah
wanted her to take music lessons, and pa-
pah was very particular who she went out
with, and ma-mah was worried whenever
she stayed out after twelve. I did n't want
to call her down, but I could tell from the
dress and the talk and all that that she'd
never had any diamonds to throw at the
birds. But then I was spinnin' pipe dreams
myself, tellin' about how much I lose on
the board and all that."

Miller leaned back in his chair and
roared. Artie waited for him to subside.

" I took her home, but not all the way.
She stopped on the corner and said that

was far enough. I sized it up that the house was on the bum and she did n't want me to see it. I had her name and I told her I wanted to write to her. She said, ' Mebbe,' and then she flew."

" Did n't you kiss her good-night ? " asked young Mr. Hall, roguishly.

" Well, the ——," and what Artie then and there said under an extreme stress of indignation need not be repeated. " Say, do you know who I 'm talkin' about? Do n't you make none o' them funny plays at me. I 'm tellin' you that this is the first time I met her. I do n't know how they act in your set, but this girl — well, you 've got to know her awhile."

" I was just joking," said young Mr. Hall.

" All right, drop it. As I was sayin', I told her I 'd write to her, but I did n't. Well, one day on Dearborn street, who does I meet but the girl, comin' out of a buildin' where all them printin' offices are.

ARTIE

'Hello, there, little one,' I says. 'Do you work up here?' That kind o' staggered her. So she weakened and said she did. She ain't a very good liar. I walked down to the corner with her and give her a little song about thinkin' all the more of her since I'd learned she was a workin' girl. She was so square I could n't string her no more, so I told her who I was and fixed it up to take her to a show. Well, when I went out to the house it was a purty small place in behind a grocery store. Pa-pah had on a woolen shirt and was smokin' a pipe. You could see that Mamie was the main screw o' the house and run things to suit herself. The old man's a hard-workin' old boy, and I think I'm strong with him. The old lady's a little leary of me, but I can win her all right."

"Is Mamie the one that you've been calling 'the girl' all the time?" asked Miller.

"She's the only one that got a Christmas present from me. And say," he continued, lowering his voice so that young Mr. Hall could not hear, "if I ever rent a flat she's the party that picks out the furniture. That ain't no josh, neither."

POOL SHARK

IV

Both Artie and Miller had been kept at the office unusually late because of the extra work that comes at the end of the month. It was nine o'clock when they left. Miller took Artie by the arm and led him toward a billiard hall, where they frequently had fifteen-ball pool contests.

Artie was the better player and usually had to "spot" three.

The corner table was not in use. With the remark that he would proceed to play pool as "old folks" played it, Artie removed his coat, pushed his linen cuffs into one of the sleeves, lighted a fat cigar and began a critical inspection of the cues in the rack. Having selected a cue he carefully deposited his cigar at one edge of the table and "busted" the fifteen balls with a fierce stroke.

When the balls stopped rolling they were scattered all over the table, but not one of them had gone into a pocket.

"A dead rank Jonah," muttered Artie, as he backed away from the table and took a firm bite at his cigar.

When he became deeply interested in a game of pool, and particularly when he was behind in the count, he dropped his usual talkative mood and became silently earnest and watchful.

Miller appeared to have caught a winning stroke, and, although Artie was expected to "spot" three, Miller had four balls before Artie made one. Then Artie became actually serious, pulling his cigar still deeper into his mouth and studying the situation carefully before undertaking a shot.

He did not observe the young man who had drifted over from another table to watch the game until this young man said, in comment on one of Artie's fail-ures: " That 's where you ought to have made a bank."

Artie glanced at him sharply. The young man had a dark mustache, pointed at the ends. His garments bespoke a sporty cheapness and he was smoking a cigarette.

Artie looked at Miller and said: " I wish I knew where I could get some brainy guy to gi' me lessons on this game."

The young man smoking the cigarette pretended not to hear this remark. He leaned against one of the posts and idly watched Miller prepare to make an impos-sible shot.

Strange to say, Miller made the impos-sible shot, although the ball did not go into the pocket for which he had vaguely intended it. Miller bore up calmly, as if he were not surprised.

" Oh, sister," moaned Artie, " I got no

ARTIE

show for my life with a man that plays
like that. Just shut your eyes every time
and you 've got a cinch."

" That was a lucky play," observed the
stranger.

" Oh, I do n't know," said Artie,
regarding the stranger with a sidewise
glance. " I do n't know."

Miller shot again and went out.

" Now, let 's make it a three-handed
game," said the stranger, coming forward.

Artie stopped short, slowly rubbed his
chin and looked at the intruder. " You
won 't think I 'm too fly if I ask you a
question, will you ? "

" Why, no."

" Well, where did you get your chips to
come in here ? I ain't seen no one
haulin' at you to get you in. Your
clothes ain't tore, as I can see."

" Now, there 's no need of makin' a
roar," said the stranger, with a conciliating
smile.

34

ARTIE

" Ain 't there ?   You 're just tryin' to
break into the game, that 's all.   I s'pose
you 're lookin' for cigarette money."

" Oh, well, if you 're goin' to act that
way I do n't care whether I play with you
or not.   I just thought ——"

" Drop it!   Do n't try to con me with
no such talk.   I 'm on to you bigger 'n a
house.   I know about you and the whole
push o' ringers.   Me and my friend here
play a gentleman's game, understand?   I
might stand some show against you, only
I do n't take my meals off of a pool table.
I ain't no shark that hangs around these
places all day lookin' for somethin' easy,
and I 'm just foolish enough to think that
I 'm too good to play pool with a skin like
you."

" Oh, you make me tired," said the
intruder, who had walked away a few
paces and then returned, as he evidently did
not wish to retreat while he was under fire.

" Is that so ? " demanded Artie, who still

35

had his cigar in his mouth. " W'y, say,
I 'll make book right here that you 're
livin' off o' your mother or sister and
payin' no board. I know you kind o'
geezers like a book. I do n't come in
here to give coin to no such stiffs as you.
No — no — not if I 'm on to my job."

" I guess you 've said about enough,"
remarked the young man with the mustache. His cigarette trembled between
his stained fingers.

" Mebbe — but I 'm in purty good voice
yet, if any one should ask. I just want
to put you next to one thing. When any
o' you blokies try to push into a game
where I am and get me to put up any
dough against your shark combinations —
w'y, you 're on a dead one. I may be a
farmer, but it takes better people than you
to sling the bull con into me."

The stranger turned half-way around
and said : " I do n't care to quarrel with
you in here. I 'll see you later."

ARTIE

Then he started to walk away.

" Mebbe you will," said Artie, "but you won't be lookin' for me, you big stiff."

And with that he began digging his cuffs out of his coat-sleeve.

" How was it ? " he asked, grinning at Miller.

" I thought he was going to fight."

" Not that boy.   He was four-flushin'. I know the brand."

V

It was not a strange thing, after all —
the growing friendship between Miller and
Artie.

There is a common theory, and a theory
at best, that "birds of a feather flock
together," and this may mean that the
human being selects for his companions
the people who are much like himself in
tastes, habits and aspirations.

Nevertheless, a South Side man, who
has written a large book intended to be a
guide to happiness and sold by subscription
only, claims that a tall man should marry
a short woman, a blonde should select a
brunette, the quiet man should choose for
his partner a vivacious woman and the
intellectual giant should give the prefer-
ence to a housekeeper or a cook.

O' THEM RAH-RAH BOYS

ARTIE

He points out the obvious disadvantages that would result were an artist to be tied up with an art critic, and depicts the misery obtaining in that household every member of which wishes to do all the talking.

Miller and Artie got along famously together. Miller was the listener and Artie was the entertainer. Miller read books and Artie read the town.

Miller secretly believed that Artie was a superficial young man, but he had to admire his candor and his worldly cleverness. Artie liked Miller because he was a font of sympathy and accepted a confidence in a serious way.

Miller knew only one kind of people, and these were the three-button-cutaway, standing-collar, derby-hat people of his own reputable station in life.

Artie had acquaintances in every layer of society.

Artie's casual reflections on matters about town were so many revelations to

39

ARTIE

Miller, whose ignorance, considering that he belonged to a club and had a library of his own, was appalling. Artie's ordinary experiences were thrilling adventures and Artie's love affairs and the briskness with which they were conducted, amazed and interested him.

Miller had always lacked the resolution to have any love affairs of his own.

At the close of an unusually dull day in the office Miller and Artie went to a "new place" to eat. It was a dull week when Artie could not find a new restaurant, and he was especially warm in his praise of this latest discovery, because it offered a complete dinner for the comparatively small sum of fifty cents.

Artie had been in a bad humor all day and had taken out his spite on young Mr. Hall, who had been lolling at his desk throughout the afternoon and writing a long letter to a chum who was attending a school somewhere in the east.

" Who is he—one o' them rah-rah boys with a big bunch o' hair?" asked Artie when young Mr. Hall first spoke of the " chum."

"He's an awfully nice fellow," responded young Mr. Hall, stiffly. He had attended the academy himself and he did not like the reference to " rah-rah boys."

" I'll bet he's one o' them saucy guys that wears a big ribbon. Say, you skipped a couple o' pages there."

Young Mr. Hall, after filling the first page of his letter, had begun writing on the fourth page. He paid no attention to Artie's sarcasm. After he had filled the last page he opened the sheet and began inside, writing crosswise of the paper.

Artie, who had been watching with cold disgust, said: " When your old college chum gets that letter it'll keep him guessin' where to begin on it."

Young Mr. Hall smiled rather con

temptuously. " Did n't you ever see a letter written this way?" he asked.

" Certainly not.   I 've been gettin' letters right along from the nicest people on the South Side and they always begin on the last page and write it backwards.   On the level, I 'm surprised you ain't on to that.   Anybody that 'd write that kind of letter could n't play in our set."

" For goodness' sake, stop!" exclaimed young Mr. Hall.   " You 're getting me so rattled I can't write."

" W'y, sure, only I was tryin' to put you next to some good pointers.   I do n't like to see a nice promisin' boy like you queer himself in sassiety just when he 's at the post."

" What do you know about society?" demanded young Mr. Hall.

" Why, Harold, old chap, I know all about it — I know it easy, too.   Did n't you see me at the last charity ball?"

" I 'd like to see you at a charity ball,"

said young Mr. Hall, derisively. He was becoming thoroughly exasperated.

"Oh, I could be there, I guess, if I wanted to. It's a case o' ten bucks and rentin' one o' them waiter suits. I know boys that went down there and put on a dizzy front, and next day they had to make a hot touch for a short coin so as to get the price of a couple o' sinkers and a good old 'draw one.'"

"Well, that's all right: let me finish my letter."

"Go ahead, old fel, I never said a word."

But he kept on nagging the unhappy young man just the same, and Miller wondered at it, for he had never before seen Artie in such an ugly mood.

Therefore, when they had reached the restaurant and Artie continued to be glum and unsociable, Miller asked him the direct question : "What's the matter with you, anyway ?"

"O, nothin' much. On the hog, that's

al. Been feelin' rotten all day. I ain't
going to tell you at the office, but it's a
off with me and the gal."

"Who! Mamie?"

"That's the name, all right. She was
up in the air. She did n't do a thing,
was a great big crank to ever go chasin
after her in the first place. On the square
Miller, I can't get wise to a girl. To
deep, too deep. Just when you thin
you 've got everything nailed down — bing
and it 's all off, see?"

Miller admitted that he did n't exactly
see. "Have you quarreled?" he asked.

"Here, I 'll give you the whole busi
ness. I goes out there last night, go
there about nine o'clock, and who does
meet comin' out o' the house but a chea
gazzabo that was with her the first time
see her. I 've told you, ain't I, how
snared her away from him?"

"Yes; his name was Wilson."

"Same boy. I told you what he was -

44

a horrible Reub; one o' them fellows that you want to get a crack at the minute you see him. You kind o' feel there 's a crack comin' to him. Mame opens the door, and I goes in — purty chilly, too. 'Who 's your friend?' I says. She puts on as good a front as she can and says, 'That 's Mr. Wilson that was up to the dance that night.' 'Well,' I says, 'he must be a peach to come around here after the way you turned him down.' She tries to pass it off, and says so-and-so and so-and-so about him bein' soft and writin' notes to her all the time. 'Come off,' I says; 'he would n't be writin' notes and comin' 'round here unless he had some pull.'"

"I do n't know about that, Artie," suggested Miller. "Just because a fellow calls on a girl is no sign that she likes him."

"Yes, but this guy 's an Indian. He won 't do. He do n't belong. It made me crazy to think he 'd been cuttin' in there. Mame tried to give me a con talk and that made me sore. 'Look here,' I says, ' I play no understudy to a low card. Now, if you 're stuck on him I 'll cash in right here and drop out o' the game.' She said she was n't stuck on him, but she could n't tell him to keep away from the house. ' If I ever find him here you won't need to tell him,' I says. ' I 'll dig into him and tear him to strips.' Then she says : ' Just because I've got other gentlemen friends ain't no call for you to walk on me.' "

" Did she say that ? "

"That's what she was gettin' at. I says : ' Nay, nay, Pauline ; your own Willie's got to be the whole thing or nothin'. An' I told her if I was beat out I wanted to be done up by somebody besides a counterfeit. Then she cried and said she 'd never speak to me again, and I says, ' Well, there are others,' and with that I goes into the hallway, takes my hat off the hook and ducks, and there you are. Everything off."

" No, not necessarily. It seems to me that you quit her, instead of her quitting you. Do n't you think you can fix it up?"

" Say, it *might* be squared," and he spoke rather hopefully, " but there 's only one way to fix it with me. That Indian 's got to keep clear off o' that street. You can make book on that."

VI

Artie and Miller had gone to a matinée on Saturday afternoon. They very seldom did this, but it was a cold and cloudy day, and on such a day the light and warmth of the play-house seemed very attractive.

After the third act they had walked out to the front of the house and were standing in the lobby, when Bancroft Walters came in very hurriedly and started toward the box office.

Bancroft Walters is the second son of LaGrange Walters, who manufactures a superior kind of roofing and has grown moderately rich at it.

Bancroft plays the banjo, appears at amateur entertainments, goes to a great many parties, and probably belongs to that

TWO-SPOT

indefinite class known as "society young
men." He has a desk in his father's
office, but it cannot be said truly that he
is held down to office hours or that his
salary represents the value of his actual
service. He attended an eastern college
for two years, and then came home for
some reason, which perhaps only his fond
and trusting mother could satisfactorily
explain.

She knows it was the fault of the college.

Bancroft is inclined to be dapper, talkative and wonderfully full of self-assur-
ance. Then he has that gift of not dis-
covering that most people regard him as a
very ordinary sort of person.

When Bancroft saw Miller and Artie
he smiled and said, " Hello, men."

" Why, how do you do, Mr. Walters ?"
replied Miller.

Artie said nothing.

Bancroft bought his seats and then

walked over to Artie and slapped him on the back.

"Well, Artie, have you seen any good mills lately?" he asked.

Artie shrugged his shoulders, tightened his lips and said nothing.

Even then young Mr. Walters did not know that trouble was breeding.

"I haven't seen you for a long time, Artie."

"I seen you since you seen me," replied Artie.

"Is that so?"

"Yes, and I want to tell you somethin', Banny. You're nothin' but a two-spot. You're the smallest thing in the deck. Say, I see barrel-house boys goin' around for hand-outs that was more on the level than you are. Now, I'll put you next to one thing; I want nothin' to do with you, because I'm on. I know you — see?"

"What do you know? What do you

mean?" Bancroft was frowning fiercely, but he was also very red.

" Chee-e-ese it! You know what I mean. You can't do nothin' like that to me and then come around afterwards and jolly me. Not in a million! I'll tell you, you're a two-spot, and if you come into the same part o' town with me I'll change your face. There's only one way to get back at you people."

" I guess I know what you're talking about now, but I do n't see that I'm called on to make any explanations," said Walters, who was recovering his voice.

" I do n't want no explanations. I pass you up. All I say is, keep away. I want to mix with white people. I'm very foolish about that, of course, but it's a way I've got. You're a nice boy, but your work is very coarse, and I'm givin' it to you right when I say that I've got a license at this minute to give you a good swift punch."

" Hold on, Artie," exclaimed Miller, seizing his friend by the arm. Miller was pale. He interfered at the right moment, for Artie's anger was up and his fist was in readiness. Walters suddenly turned up his collar and said, in a voice trembling with rage : " I'm not going to have any trouble in this kind of a place."

Then he turned and walked away with the best show of dignity at his command, while Miller still held Artie by the arm and stared at him.

For once he believed Artie to be in the wrong. Bancroft had come up and spoken pleasantly enough, and in return Artie had played the part of a bully seeking a pretext for a fight.

" What made you act that way ?" he demanded.

" Do you know that boy ?"

" Well, I 've met him."

" Yes, but you do n't half know him.

I ought o' smashed him before he opened his face."

" What 's the trouble between you ?"

" Oh, well, let it drop. He knows, though. He knows. And I think he 'll remember two or three things I told him. Come on in and let 's see the rest of the show."

They did not enjoy the last act of the play.

Artie was still simmering with indignation, and he was also worried to think that Miller had been offended. As for Miller, he could only wonder that Artie had shown such a fierce disposition to fight when there was no apparent provocation.

As they were leaving the theater Artie said : " I think I 'll just tell you why I 've got it in for that Charley boy. I ain't stuck on tellin' it, for it made me look like a monkey."

" I could n't imagine what was the

matter," said Miller. "Walters always seemed to me to be a nice sort of fellow — that is, harmless."

"Harmless? He threw the boots into me the worst I ever got 'em. Ooh! He made me feel like a tramp. Say, Miller, if I was to beat his whole face off I could n't ketch even. He got way under the skin on me. Now, this is on the q. t., but did you ever get the worst of it in such a way that you could n't come back at the time, and yet you was so crazy mad that you could 'a' cried? Well, that was me."

"I'm surprised."

"Was n't I? W'y, I went to school with that guy out on the South Side when my old man had a job in the foundry and old Walters was just beginnin' to get a little dough. The family did n't put on no such lugs in them days. But then, there's no roar comin' on that, because the old man's as common as dirt, and this same two-spot's got a sister that can have my seat in the car any time she comes in. I ain't one o' them beefers that's got it in for people just because they've got the coin and make a front with it. I'm out for the stuff myself. But I do hate to see any of 'em get swelled on account of it."

"Well, now," said Miller, "it never seemed to me that Walters was that kind."

"That's what knocked me the twister. I thought this fellow was all right. I've known him to speak to ever since we learned to smoke cigarettes together back o' the car barns. Here not more'n six months ago he comes into a restaurant where I was settin'. He was with a lot o' them Prairie avenue boys, and purty soon he ducks 'em and comes over an' touches me for two cases. Now, you know you can't go up and bone a stranger for stuff, can you? He knew me well enough to get the two."

" Did he pay it back ? "

" Sure he did. I ain't sayin' that he's crooked. I 'll tell you when he give it back to me. It was one night out at the boat club when we was havin' some bouts there. I brought over a handy boy from the West Side to put him against a little fellow from the boxin' school. They told me over west the boy was a world-beater, but, gee! this North-Sider made a choppin' block out of him. What I was goin' to get at was that Banny was there."

" Who's Banny ? "

" That's his name. We used to call him that when he was a kid. Well, he was out there that night bettin' all kinds o' talk, and you 'd thought I was his long-lost brother. He stood around the corner where I was handlin' my man, and it was ' Artie ' this and ' Artie ' that all the time. He loved me that night. Mebbe that 's because he had a few under his belt, but anyway it went with me. I thought the boy was all right."

Artie paused in his story and put a large cigar into his mouth. Miller reached into his pocket for a match, but Artie shook his head.

" This is how I found the streak o' yellow in him," said he. " One afternoon the boss sent me out to Grand Crossin' to see a man. I stayed for supper out there and was comin' in on the train along to-wards eight o'clock. At one o' them stations out there, here comes a whole crowd o' people — a lot o' swell girls and their fly boys. The car was nearly full. I 'm alone in a double seat, see ? A girl comes runnin' down the aisle and sets down right across from me and says, ' Hurry up and grab this place.' Then who comes up and drops into the seat with her but Banny, understand ? I 'm readin' the paper, but I drops it and makes the horrible play. I lifts my derby clear off o' my head ard I

ARTIE

says: 'Good evening!' Say, he was four
feet away. Say, it was just like you there
and me here. This queen with him sees
me make the play and kind o' giggles.
Mebbe I did n't do it right. But him —
he turned around sideways in his seat and
begins chinnin' her and never sees me at
all. Course, you could n't expect him to.
I was nearly three feet away and lookin'
right at him. Miller, this is straight, so
help me. He threw me down. He 'd
never seen me before. All because he
was out with the swell push and had this
queen with him. I pulled the paper up in
front o' me, and I thought my ears 'd fry
and fall off. I was groggy. Never did I
get it harder. Talk about a half-hook on
the point o' the jaw!"

"It was a confounded shame," said
Miller, warmly.

"Say, Miller, am I a vag? Am I fit
to ride on a train with other people?
Would a man queer himself by speakin'

to me? Now, I did n't expect no knock-
down to his girl. I do n't trot in her class.
But to think of that stiff turnin' on me
because I spoke to him. That 's what
put the hooks into me. I won't forget
it—never. I was sore, but it was worse 'n
that. It made me feel rotten."

"I 'm not surprised."

"Well, I did n't see him again till to-
day. You heard what I said. Well, at
that, he 's got the best of it. I never will
be able to give him the right kind of a hot
come-back for what he done to me."

VII

One Saturday afternoon Artie Blanchard was enjoying his half-holiday in a manner peculiar to himself. He was battling with the crowd in State street.

He had his coat-collar turned up and his hat was pulled rakishly forward so that it threatened to produce friction with his eyebrows every time he changed the expression of his face.

He was whistling a little composition that had lately taken possession of his thoughtful moments. It was entitled "I'll Be True to My Honey Boy."

Artie did not know the tune or the words, so he merely whistled it on speculation and when he came to the doubtful parts he hurdled.

THE CONNELLY GIRLS

ARTIE

When he grew tired of whistling he smoked a black cigar.

Artie was apparently at peace with the world and any one to have seen him shift his cigar from the right pocket of his mouth to the left merely by the play of facial muscles would have said, " Here 's a young man content."

But Artie, like many other young persons, never whistled more cheerfully, smoked more hungrily and looked into show windows with more seeming interest than when he was keeping company with a great sorrow.

It could have been nothing less than the guiding hand of Fate that shoved him around a bevy of women who were carrying bundles and looking at show windows at the same time, thus contriving to mow down anything and anybody that happened in their way. For Artie immediately got a view of the cause of his sorrow. He would have known her by the sacque alone, but the sprig of plumes on the hat helped in the identification.

Your ordinary lover would have re-treated, palpitating. Considering that when Artie had last seen her she was all tears and that his parting words had been, " There are others," it would have been proper for him to drop back into the moving crowd before she turned from the display of precious furs and saw him there looking at her.

But Artie did nothing of the kind.

He walked up to her, brushed some imaginary dust from the bulge of her sleeve, and said: " Hello, girlerino! How 's everything stackin' ? "

Mamie turned around and there was a leap of color to her face.

She said: " Why, Mr. Blanchard."

" What was you pipin' off—the furs?" asked Artie.

" Yes," with her face half-turned from him.

" Do you see the big sealskin sacque
there ? I was lookin' at it the other day.
I 'm thinkin' o' buyin' it for a lady friend
o' mine."

" Indeed ! "

By this time she had recovered somewhat and she spoke with an evident attempt to be coldly sarcastic.

" You heard me, did n't you ? I went
in and asked the main squeeze o' the works
how much the sacque meant to him, and
he said I could have it for four hundred
samoleons. ' Well,' I says, ' that 's a
mere bagatelle to me. That would n't
keep me in shirt-studs for a month.' "

He paused for a moment or two, watching her all the time, and then he said :
" But mebbe you 'd rather have that
other one up there. You know what
you 'd like."

Mamie did not look at him and she did
not answer. Artie's attempted playful-
ness was too bearish for her, and Artie

seemed suddenly to realize this. He changed his tactics.

" Mame," he said, putting his forefinger softly against her arm.

" Well ? "

" Is it fixed up ? "

"Is what fixed up?"

" You know."

" No, I do n't."

They were standing side by side, both looking intently into the show-window and talking to it. Their conduct was sufficiently strange to have attracted the attention of the people who brushed against them. But in State street the pedestrians will not give their serious attention to a man unless he does something worthy — such as falling off a cable car or colliding with the tongue of a wagon.

" How about my little old picture ? Is it turned to the wall ? "

" I — guess not."

"Oh, you 're guessin', are you ? Well, I s 'pose the other boy 's fillin' all my dates ? "

"That silly thing!"

Artie chirruped as if skeptical. "He 's a nice boy," said he, and he added, after a deep sigh, "Nit — not."

Mamie turned to him, and, in a quick flame of earnestness, said : "Artie, you know I can't bear that old thing, and I 'll never speak to him again as long as I live." She had tears in her eyes.

"You won't be loser anything at that."

"I 'm going to write to him and let him know something."

"Why, no ; not at all. I 've told you all along that if you 'd give me his address I 'd go around and fix it all up with him."

"If it had n't been for him we would n't have —— "

"Would n't have put on the gloves, eh ? Well, come on. Let 's be movin'."

ARTIE

He took her by the arm, and then he remembered that it was State street and three o'clock in the afternoon, so he let go.

"I have to meet the Connelly girls in a few minutes. I promised them."

"Shake 'em. You 've got somethin' better than the Connelly girls."

Mamie gave him a vicious nudge in the ribs and broke out laughing, and the war was then and there over, before the tears had dried.

"About Tuesday night, Mame?"

"Yes — or Monday."

"Good enough. An' now you come right in here and get into line with a bunch o' violets. There 's nothin' too rich for the sunshine o' the North Side."

It was not the same Mamie who came out of the florist's wearing violets, and it was not the same Artie who was grinning at her delight over the little present.

" Now, I must go for the Connelly
girls," said she.

" All right.   Say, Mame."

" Yes."

" I 'll just make that to-morrow night."

VIII

At eight o'clock the front room was gently baking with heat from the base-burner, and the gas-jet, with four scalloped dance programmes dangling from it, was lighted to the utmost.

On the marble-topped table was the photograph of a tense young man with plastered hair. The picture lay against a metallic prop of fanciful design which was intrenched between the album and a copy of " Lucille." The swollen furniture was ornately jig-sawed and confined in plush, and every piece of it was modestly backed up against the wall.

The crayon portrait of Mamie's father looked down benignly on this room cleared for action. The portrait represented a bearded fop with a fantastic forelock, a

HE INDIAN

neck-tie spotted with great accuracy and a shirt-front bearing a lump of gold. On two or three occasions of his life, Mamie's father had borne an approximate resemblance to the man in the frame.

One occasion was that of the visit to the photographer's and the other was that of the social reception to the executive committee of the Union. In the picture Mamie's father was clean and unwrinkled and he bore a placid, maiden-like expression which Mamie had seldom observed in him.

The crayon portrait had originally been a bargain for $2.50, and the agent who delivered it had put in a frame at $14. The frame was a boiling foliage of white and silver. With such a picture in the house there was no chance for Mamie to lose regard for her father. As for the father, he escaped an affliction of pride by remaining in other rooms of the house.

This crayon portrait dwarfed the " Yard

of Roses," the " Wide-Awake" and " Fast Asleep" prints and the other pictures hanging on the walls. It was the luminous thing of the front parlor, and it was to the portrait that Artie Blanchard addressed himself as he came in from the hallway, with his arm lingering at Mamie's waist, half-way between a caress and a hug. " Hello, old boy," said he, and then he asked Mamie, " How does the old gentleman stack up ? "

" He's back there now, reading the paper."

"All right. I was n't lookin' for him."

Artie pulled out a chair and seated himself in it sidewise. He happened to see the photograph on the table.

Artie — " Well, I 'm not turned to the wall, eh ? "

Mamie — " Do n't begin talking that way."

Artie — " I was just kiddin', Mame. How's the ma-mah ? "

ARTIE

Mamie — " She was asking about you to-day."

Artie — " Say, on the square, has she got any time for me ? "

Mamie (*warmly*) — " Why, of course. She likes you."

Artie — " Well, the ma-mah's got a cold eye in her head. I can't make out whether I'm strong or not. She ain't the kind of a girl that'd be afraid to say a few things if she wanted to."

Mamie — " Pooh ! "

Artie — " How about the ringer ? "

Mamie — " What's that ? "

Artie — " You know — that guy you was goin' to frost. Have you wrote to him ? "

Mamie (*excitedly*) — " You mean Mr. Wilson. I have n't told you, have I ? "

Artie — " Well, I should say not. Has he been trailin' you again ? "

Mamie — " No, but he wrote to me.

ARTIE

It 's the funniest thing you ever read.
I 'll get you the letter."

Artie — " Gee ! That boy 's a stayer.
If he do n't keep off o' my route there 'll
be people walkin' slow behind him one o'
these days. Let 's see what he says."

*(Mamie goes to the adjoining room and re-
turns with a letter and offers it to Artie.)*

Artie — " Go on and spiel."

Mamie (*with a nervous giggle as a pre-
liminary*) — " Well, he begins by saying,
' Miss Mary Carroll, My Dear Madam.' "

Artie — " ' 'My Dear Madam.' Would n't
that cook you, though ? "

Mamie — " Listen." (*Reads*)

" I do not know why you should have
treated me as you have done. I have always
regarded you as a friend, but of late I have come
to the opinion that you desire to sever our
friendship, seeing that you did not speak when
I met you last Sunday eve. If you have
anything against me I would like to know in
what regards I have not treated you right and

72

like a lady.   I am very truly, your obedient
servant.   GRANT WILSON."

Artie — "That's a good thing.   I
wonder where he got next to that fancy
pass about severin' friendships.   I'll make
that foxy boy think somebody's severed
him if I take a crack at him.   Did you
answer it, Mame?"

Mamie — "Not yet.   Would you?"

Artie — "Sure!   I'd send him one
that'd burn a hole in the mail-sack.   You
get your little old sheet of paper and I'll
tip you off a few things to tell that boy.
I'll bet you all kinds of money that I
can send him somethin' that he'll talk
about in his sleep.   You get the paper."

(*Mamie goes to the next room and returns
with writing material.   She removes the
photograph album and then seats herself at
the table ready to write.   An attack of the
giggles.*)

Artie — "Chop the laughin'.   Go on
and write to him.   I'll tell you what to

say. Just begin this way, ' You 're all right but you won't do.' "

Mamie — " No, no, Artie, please no. I do n't want to say it that way. Besides, I 've got to address him first. Now, what shall I call him ? "

Artie — " You could call him a good many things and make no error, I 'll tell you those."

Mamie — " I know, but shall I say ' Mr. Wilson, Sir,' or just ' Dear Sir ? ' "

Artie — "Naw, not in a thousand. What do you want to jolly him for ? Get in plenty o' rough work right from the start. Throw it into him hard. Call him ' foolish Wilson boy.' You 've got to wallop one o' them people to make 'em understand. Just say, ' Get out o' town and keep quiet and you may live to see the flowers again.' If you give him that easy talk he 'll think you 're leadin' him on. Let *me* write to his nobs and *I'll* fix him. (*Artie takes the pen and writes for a*

ARTIE

few moments, Mamie watching him and suppressing giggles.) Now, how's this? This is the real stuff. (*Reads.*)

" ' I just received your nervy letter. You are all right, but you won't do. Do not come into our ward or I will have you pinched. Remember, I never saw you before in all my life. You are worse than a stranger to me. I would advise you to stop smokin' that double-X brand of dope, because it gives you funny dreams. By fallin' off the earth you will oblige.' "

Mamie (*on the verge of hysterics*) — " Oh-h-h-h-h ! What *would* he think if I sent him a letter like that ?"

Artie — " He 'd think he was up against the cold outside, and that 's where he is, huh ?"

Mamie — " Of course. You know that."

(*Artie drops the pen, and with great caution wraps his arm around her waist.*)

TABLEAU.

75

IX

On that morning Artie had come in a half-hour late.

His " Good morning, people," was dry and husky, and after he had seated himself at his desk he put his left palm up to his forehead, sighed deeply, and said, without addressing any one in particular: " The boy that wrote that song about ' Oh, what a difference in the morning,' was on to his job. I 've got a set o' coppers on me this g. m. that 'd heat a four-room flat and my mouth tastes like a Chinese family 'd just moved out of it."

"Another poker party ? " asked Miller.

" Guess again. Worse 'n any poker party. A bat — a real old bat. Pazoo-oo-oom! Ooh! Mebbe you think I ain 't got a lulu of a head on me this morning.

76

THE BATTLE-AX

ARTIE

I ought to be out at the Washin'tonian home with the rest o' them stills and hypos."

"You do n't mean to say that you were — loaded ?" inquired Miller, leaning over his desk and lowering his voice so that young Mr. Hall should not hear.

"To the guards. Up to here," and Artie, elevating his chin, drew a forefinger across his Adam's apple.

"Well, I declare," said Miller, and in his voice were both sorrow and reproof.

"Jump on to me," said Artie, as he tried to rub the sleep out of his eyes. "You can't make me feel any sorer 'n I was when I woke up this morning. My head reached out over two pillows. I did n't do a thing to the water pitcher, neither. When I tossed that water into me it sounded like when a blacksmith sticks a red-hot horseshoe into a tub of water. That 's no dream, neither."

"How did it happen ?"

ARTIE

" How does any o' them things happen?
After playin' three or four games o' pool
I starts out to get a car and I ain't got
it yet. That's always the way — good
thing, too. Say, Miller, there ain't many
men that go out huntin' a tide. It's a
case of meetin' a friend and him sayin'
somethin', and then another friend and he
loosens, and then you come up, and then
the first man thaws again and nobody
wants to welch on the proposition, and
they keep comin' along and you 're a good
fellow, see? and do n't want to be a quitter, and the first thing you know you 're
up against it, and you do n't care whether
there 's any night cars runnin' or not."

" Is that what happened last night ? "

" About it. I meets Billy Munster,
and if you ever trotted a heat with him
you know that he 's one o'f the biggest
jolliers that ever come over the hills, and
when it comes to bowlin' — well, he pours
a drink that 'd make any bar-tender quit

bein' sociable. Did you ever try his game ? "

" I never heard of him."

" You 've missed a whole lot. He 's got a job over at the city hall. I never see him do a stroke of work, but he can always make a flash o' the long green, and I guess it 's easy money, too, from the way he lets go of it. I 've heard he gets his bit on nearly every good thing that comes along. What his pull is I never could figure out. Every time I see him over at the city hall he 's whisperin' to one o' them red-necked boys and fixin' it up to give somebody the double-cross. At that, he 's a good fellow. I think he 'd mace a sucker if he got half a chance, but after he got the dough he 'd spend it freely. That's the kind of a boy he is, and last night he had a roll that you could 'a' stopped up a window with. The minute I meets him he steers me into a joint, makes me heave in a couple and then says: 'Come on; I've got a good thing for you.' ' Nit,' I says, because I knew his gait. I says: ' I 've seen enough o' them sunrises over old Lake Michigan.' ' No,' he says ; ' on the level; we 'll just drop into the music hall and stay a little while.' So I goes."

" You ought to have gone on home."

" Sure ; we all know that the next day. But I goes just the same. We had n't been in there ten minutes till Billy dug up a 'longshoreman with gold in her teeth and was buyin' beer for her. He kept 'em comin' fast and I could n't dodge 'em. Purty soon I was joinin' in the chorus, and I guess from that stage o' the game they did n't have to pull at me to keep me up and comin.' When the song-bird come out to do her turn I could see two of her. I guess this girl that Billy knew spotted us for a couple of easy marks, for she floated away somewhere and come back with a friend o' hers."

ARTIE

Artie stopped in his narrative and gave a low, buzzing whistle. " You ought to seen her."

" Why ? " asked Miller, and he had to smile in anticipation.

" Say, there was a battle-ax if ever you see one. She had a face on her that 'd fade flowers. It had one o' them calcimine hard finishes. You can guess how far along I was when I did n't shy at it. And oh, the haughty front that she put up. She said she was an actorine. ' What troupe ? ' I says. ' Well,' she says, ' at present I 'm restin'.' I 'll bet a dollar she never done nothin' on the stage but carry a shield, but to hear the guff she was throwin' out you 'd think she could make Ellen Terry look like a Friday night amatoor. Oh, she was a bird. I think her name was Gladys. If she come in this room now I 'd jump out o' that window, and last night when I was sloppy I thought she was the best ever. That just goes

ARTIE

to show what the hop-juice 'll do for you."

" How long did you stay there ? "

" Till the whole works was closed. I bought drinks for this pelican friend o' mine till she hollered for me to stop, and then I says to Billy, I says : ' Let 's take the ladies out and give 'em a little supper.' That was me said that, understand ? It was only a little after midnight, you know—the mere shank o' the evening—and I could n't think o' startin' home as early as that. Oh, no. Little Artie had to go and give the ladies some supper. You know how liberal a guy is about that time o' night. He do n't like to take no money home with him. Billy was right with me, of course. He 's a stayer from Stayersville. We got out o' the music hall — I remember that — and the next thing I can cipher out was that we got to the restaurant and I was pleadin' with my tall friend to just go right ahead

ARTIE

and order anything she wanted. Well,
she was fly enough to do that. Little
Gladys was more 'n seven. I think it 'd be
about an even-money break that she 's
seven times seven. She ordered nearly
everything on the bill and I guess I went
to sleep with my face in a plate. That 's
after Billy had ordered two or three more
rounds. Oh, he 's a wonder, that boy.
I do n't know where he stows it."

Artie took a full breath and once more
felt of his head.

"That 's about all I remember," said
he, "except payin' the check and havin'
Billy take me over to the hotel. It must
'a' been three o'clock when I got to bed
and I pounded my ear till past seven.
I 've had a nice breakfast. It was a tall
tub o' seltzer lemonade. Talk about
old R. E. Morse; I 'm full of it this
morning. This is the first time I 've had
a day-after head in many moons, and if
you ever ketch me with another one you

83

can take a ball club and hammer the life out o' me. Now, that goes."

"What do you think Mamie would say if she knew you had been out with this other girl?" asked Miller, rather severely.

"Stop it, Miller. Do n't go to rubbin' it in. I got trouble enough to-day without thinkin' o' that. If she 'd ever saw me with that fairy I would n't be deuce high with her now. You could n't blame her neither. What do you think of a chump that 'd pass up a four-time winner to go and play his money against a sellin' plater, and a has-been at that? I did n't put you on to the good thing though, did I? Last night I had nine cases. This morning when I frisked myself I could n't turn up only sixty cents. I just fed eight big iron louies into that game last night. I do n't know how I 'll ever keep up the bluff o' workin' to-day. How do I look?"

"You look knocked out."

"Well, I feel the part."

. CARROLL

X

"I've got it to do," said Artie, "and
I s'pose I'd better put on the best front
I can and play it out."

"There's nothing to be afraid of,"
suggested Miller.

"Do n't tell me nothin' about that
game. I know just what it'll be. On
the dead, I'd give a ten-case note to be
out of it, but Mame would n't have it
that way. She said she'd promised the
Connelly girl, and there you are. I'm
goin' to be the head knocker in the push.
It's a case of gettin' a day off and seein'
the thing through from soda to hock. We
got to meet at the house and go from there
in a carriage."

"You'll enjoy it," said Miller, smiling.

"What, doin' the slow march up the

aisle and then standin' there while the
main guy spiels and all that business?
Not on your tintype. I'll make a mis-
cue somewhere; you see if I do n't."

" You 'd better get used to it and find
out how it 's done. Some of these
days you 'll have to go through the mill
yourself."

" Say, that 's what I told Mame, and
you ought o' seen her. She blushed up
and got rattled and could n't say a word."

" She understood what you meant,
did n't she ? "

" Well, I guess she was keen enough
to make a good, warm guess at it."

Miller gazed at Artie for a few moments
and then said: " It 's none of my business,
Artie, but — you two are engaged, are n't
you ? "

Artie swallowed something and seemed
to be considerably embarrassed.

" Miller," said he, confidentially, "you 've
asked me a hard one. On the level, I

do n't know whether we 've got it fixed up or not. You know my style of play. I can kid all right, but when it comes to makin' a dead serious play I 'm a horrible frost. I 'm the worst that ever come up the pike. Between you and me and the desk here, I think she knows that it 's goin' to be a marry as soon as things come right. But as for me ever comin' to the scratch and sayin', ' Here, how it is ? Do you want to open my mail ? ' w'y, I never had the face to do it yet."

" I thought you had nerve enough to do anything."

" Miller, let me put you next to some-thin'. I know a bad man on the West Side that can lick his weight in wildcats and bluff any four or five common dubs, and he 's got a wife that weighs about ninety pounds that 'll give him just one look and he 'll crawl under a table. He 's dead stuck on her, and she can do anything she wants to with him. It ain't that he

ain 't got nerve enough. What is it, then?
Huh?"

" You 're getting too deep for me,
Artie," said Miller, shaking his head.
" What I meant was that I thought you
knew Mamie so well you could be perfectly free and candid with her."

" I 'm an easy runner till it comes to the
high jump and then I quit cold. I
can jolly and have fun and put my
arm around her, but when it comes
to takin' her by the mit and doin' the
straight talk — nit, and again nit. Two
or three times here lately I 've said to
myself : ' W'y, you big stiff, brace up
and get through with it before you go
daffy.' Then I think I 'm all right, see?
But as soon as I get with her all that
brace fades on me and I say : ' What 's
the good? Next week 'll do just as well.'
Besides, would n't I make a picture if
she 'd stand me off?"

" It seems to me that when she asked

you to stand up with her at this wedding that was about as strong a hint as you could ask. You do n't expect her to come right out, do you ? "

" No, but I feel a good deal like a guy that I meet out at the boat club. He says that if he asked a girl to marry him and she said 'yes,' he 'd begin to think her judgment was purty rotten. I do n't s'pose anybody on top of earth can beat my time with Mame, but what she sees in me to get stuck on is what keeps your Willie boy guessin'. "

" What does any woman see in any man ? " asked Miller, gravely, somewhat gratified that Artie had taken up with a social theme of such magnitude.

" Sometimes she sees a roll o' the long green," replied Artie, " but Mame must have good eyesight if she can find any pile belongin' to me. You can turn them X rays on to my bank-book and not find enough dough to fit up a flat."

" She 's not after your money."

" No, you can gamble she ain't. I
s'pose it 's because I 'm young and good."

" Yes, because you never drink or stay
out nights."

" Break away! I 'm tryin' to forget
all about that. That 's one reason I give
in to Mame on this weddin' proposition.
I felt so ornery about the night that me
and Munster laid open the town that I 'd
'a' done most anything to get even with
myself. She said the Connelly girl and
her had gone to school together and
had been travelin' as a team, and that
Florence would n't have nobody else to
play first mate when the thing was pulled
off. And she says: ' You do n't want
nobody else to stand up with me, do
you ?' That kind o' jolted, and I told
her I was n't stuck on puttin' in an understudy, and so I promised to go agains'
the game."

ARTIE

" Do you know this girl that 's to be married ? "

" I 've seen her two or three times, but she always had the mash along. The two of 'em went with Mame and me over to Turner Hall one night. Oh, but they was gone on each other. His name 's Tommy Bradshaw and he runs a cigar store. They say he does a nice little business and be-longs with the real boys, but every time I ever see him he was a lobster. You could n't drag him more 'n six feet away from his sure thing. He kept tab on her every minute. He 'd set there holdin' her fan and whisperin' to her, and he did n't want no one else to cut in. I thought his work was very coarse. There 's no need of a man goin' nanny just because he 's copped out a nice girl all for him-self."

" Well, Artie, when a man 's in love you can 't hold him accountable."

" That 's no dream, neither. Any one that 's got his head full o' the girl proposition 's liable to go off his trolley at the first curve. I would n't 've believed it six months ago, but if that North Side wonder 'd turn on me now and gi' me the marble heart, I tell you it 's a safe money guess that I 'd go and jump in the lake."

" Yes, and your old friend Wilson would be back courting Mamie."

" Yes, he would, would he ? If she ever passes me up it 'll be for some guy that hau's a good deal more freight than that Indian does."

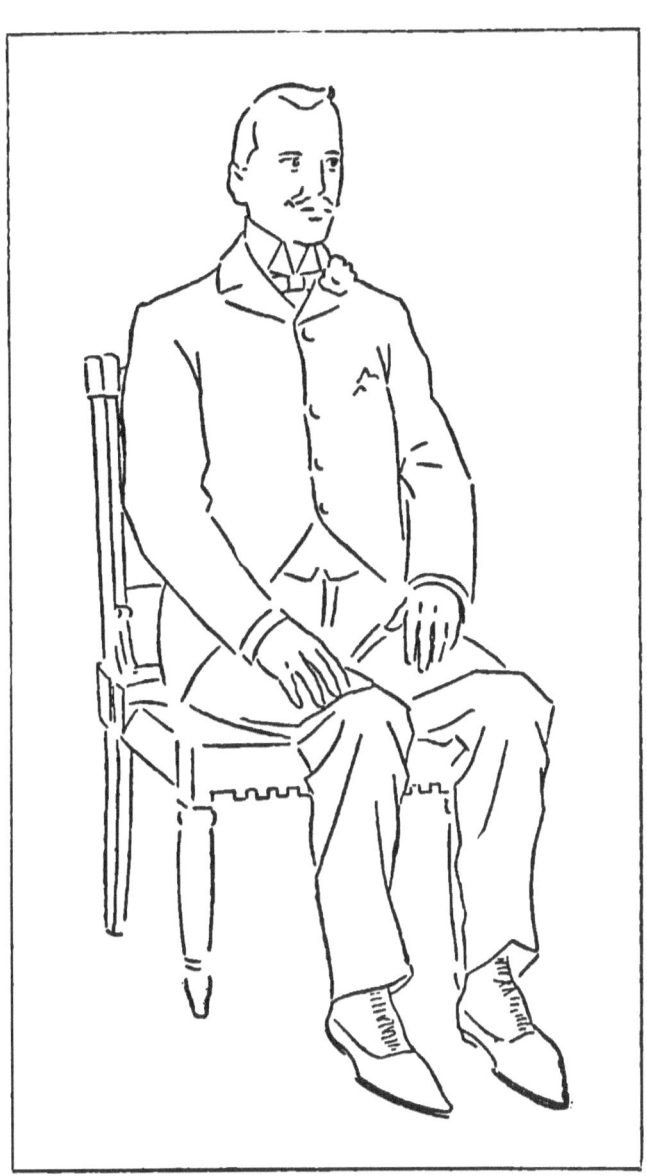

OMMY

XI

A large yellow rose drooped from Artie's lapel as he came into the office on Thursday morning.

"Hark, I think I hear them weddin' bells.
Tingaly-ting, tingaly-ting, ting-ting-ting."

As he sung this, he put one hand behind his ear and stood in the listening attitude so commonly affected by neat song-and-dance artists.

"Aha! The best man, I believe?" said Miller, moving back from his desk and regarding Artie's specialty with keen delight.

"You know it," replied Artie, "you know it. I was the stroke oar at the doin's, and while I ain't throwin' any bouquets at myself I must say that me and Mame was the hit o' the piece."

93

" You got through all right, then ? "

" A little slow on the get-away, but I made a Garrison finish. I was runnin' in strange company, too, but as soon as I got the pace they could n't head me."

" Tell me all about it. You and Mamie really stood up with them, did you ? "

" Did we ? Ain't I tellin' you that we done the pacemakin'? I give Mame a wad o' roses that laid over anything the bride could flash, and mebbe you think she was n't in good form. Oh, doctor ! She looked out o' sight ! Some of 'em have got their sealskins and their sparklers, but this little girl, with that new make-up and the flowers, beat the best of 'em. I 'll back her against all comers, bar none. Talk about your peaches, why, she 's a whole orchard ! That 's no Hungarian joke, neither."

" By George, Artie, you are hard hit," said Miller, laughing.

" You 're dead right there, an' I make

no bones about it. She's got me landed
and strung. Say, you must think I'm a
prize gilly to set around here and give up
my insides to you about her, but I'll tell
you, Miller, you're the only man that I'd
tell some things to, and I cough up to you
because I know that you're a good fellow
— and understand that — puttin' aside all
this kid talk ——"

" That's all right, Artie. You need n't
be afraid of me telling any one. There is
nothing to be ashamed of, anyway. Every
man falls in love sooner or later."

" Love! There's a word that makes
me weary, but on the square, that's
what I've got. It's a sure-enough case.
Where's Hall?"

" I think he's out collecting to-day."

" I'm glad of it. I do n't like to say
too much in front o' that boy. He do n't
know any more 'n the law allows, and since
he's started to that dancin' school I think
he hears funny noises under his bonnet."

ARTIE

"Are you going to tell me about that wedding?" asked Miller, impatiently.

"Well, it was a bird. We did n't break into the sassiety notes, but that cuts no ice in our set. It took all day to pull it off. Mame told me to come straight to the Connelly house, because she had to go there early in the morning. Her and the other Connelly girl was handlin' the bride. It was nearly ten o'clock when I got there, and there was a big push in the front room — Mame's mother, old man Connelly, Mrs. Connelly, Tommy Bradshaw — he was the main guy, you know — one o' Tommy's brothers from the South Side and a chilly mug by the name of Parker, some relation to Tommy. This frosty party was doin' the touch-me-not business all day, an' you could n't get him to take his gloves off. Tommy — new suit, new white necktie, new dicer, new shoes. When he 'd lean back and throw one leg over the other,

96

ARTIE

just to show that he was takin' it dead
easy, you could see the yellow soles o' them
shoes. He was washed and combed till
he did n't look right. Say, you could smell
the bay-rum clear across the room. I
think he overdone it, myself. And say,
you ought o' seen him when Mame's
mother started to throw the harpoon into
him."

" The harpoon ?" inquired Miller. He
had known Artie for a long time, but
occasionally the boy was too versatile for
him.

" Sure, the stringin' business. That
old girl 's a wonder. You see, here was
Mrs. Connelly settin' there snifflin' and
drippin' around as if she was goin' to bury
the daughter instead of stakin' her to a
cigar store. That worried old man Connelly, and so Mame's mother tried to jolly
the crowd up by playin' horse with
Tommy. She 'd say : ' Well, Mr. Bradshaw, you 're a very handsome man in

your new clothes,' and then throw me the
wink. Then she 'd ask him if he 'd back
out if he had the chance and how many
girls he 'd been engaged to before. She
had him balled up till he could n't say
a word. No use, though; Mrs. Connelly kept moppin' her eyes and every
little while sayin' 'Ah-h-h-h,' like that.
I guess it was n't put on, though. She
was probably broke up. Women are
different."

" Oh, yes," assented Miller, " she hated
to lose her daughter."

" I do n't believe it was that. She
claimed it was the happiest day of her life,
and then as soon as she said it she com-
menced to leak again. But you ought 'o
seen old man Connelly. Oh, he 's a
great old tad — has charge o' the wagons
for one o' them Franklin street wholesale
houses. They say he makes good money.
Well, yesterday he was up against a new
proposition. He was all togged out and

ARTIE

had a collar that was chokin' the life out
of him. All he could do was to wipe his
mouth on the back of his mit and kind o'
trail after the others. What do you think?
At the church he wanted to slide into a
back seat and let the rest of us go up
front. 'Come on,' I says; 'be a good
fellow and stay with us.' He said he
could see all right from where he was,
but his wife yanked him out and made
him stick."

   " When did you get to the church ? "

   " It was after twelve o'clock, all right.
W'y, we give a parade — three carriages
we had. I had n't hardly had a chance
to see Mame in her new clothes till we
got in the carriage with Florence and
Tommy. Florence had about twenty
yards o' this mosquito-bar stuff hangin'
to her and was made up great, but even
at that she could n't get better 'n place
with Mame in the runnin'. She 's a nice
girl, though. I do n't want to back-cap

99

ARTIE

her. She was rattled and so was Tommy.
All the way to the church they did n't say
more 'n twenty words, and that was about
how glad she was the sun had come out
and wantin' to know if Mr. Parker was
in the carriage behind. Tommy grinned
and looked foolish. To tell the truth I
got kind o' nanny myself when we stopped in front of the church and piled out.
Mame was all right, though. She froze
to me and steered me through without an
error. There was a wait just inside when
old man Connelly balked on 'em, but
after that everything went smooth. About
a dozen ringers followed us in and stood
around rubberin'."

"Well, what did you have to do?"
inquired Miller, with growing interest.

"I done nothin' but stick to Mame.
All but us four got planted in front seats
and looked on. There was a long spiel
by the high guy in the pulpit, and we
shifted two or three times, and that 's about

all I know, except that Tommy agreed to
a lot o' business that's enough to set any
boy a-thinkin' if he goes against the game.
Oh, I forgot.   It was right in the dead
serious part, just when Florence and
Tommy put their lunch-hooks together.
' They're off,' I whispered to Mame, and
she came purt' near bustin' out and queerin'
the whole act.   She roasted me good and
hard for it afterwards."

"What did you do after the ceremony?"

" Say, the ceremony was just the first
part o' the show.   When we got out o'
the church Florence's mother was cryin'
again and kissin' everybody except me and
the old man.   We ducked on her.   They
loaded up the carriages again and all but
us four went back to the house.   We
went over to get some photographs."

"Oh, I see."

" Well, I should say so.   You've always got to have one o' them bride-and-
groom pictures in the house whether

there's anything to chew or not. They
wanted me and Mame to go along, so we
rode over and watched 'em. Tommy was
all right by that time. He'd got his nerve
back, and he was real Charley-horse,
joshin' me and Mame, and sayin : ' That's
all right. Some time I'll come and see
you two hitched up.' Was n't that a raw
deal, huh ? There I was — I'd never
said nothin' to Mame about the marry
deal, and he was takin' it for granted that
everything was set. He was too new
about it. I never did like his work. But
Mame—say, she passed it off smoother'n
silk. She just give him the ha-ha and
says : ' That 'll be all right. You 'll get
your bid when the shootin' match comes
off.' "

"She did n't call it a 'shooting-
match' ? "

"Naw ! I'm just tellin' you, you know.
Well, they got their pictures, her a settin'
down with the flowers in her lap and him

ARTIE

standin' behind with one of his fins kind
o' hid in that mosquito bar. Then we all
drove back to the house to feed our faces."

" Oh, you had a wedding dinner ? "

" Did we ? That was where I cut
loose. That was where I got good. I
made a speech, just for a kid, you know,
but it started 'em — all but that cold guy. I
did n't get away till nine o'clock. We
fed an' then we smoked and danced, and
old man Connelly played the flute — rotten,
thank you. Mame was the star, too.
Do n't forget it. Honest, we had a
good time. Them people up there's good
enough for me. No frills, but they're on
the level, and when it comes down to cases
they're just as good as a lot of people that
make a bigger front. They got hearts in
the right place. It's like a man out at
the boat club says, 'If you can't travel
with the bell-cows, why stick to the gang.'
That's wise talk, too."

XII

After a hurried luncheon at one of the places where patrons help themselves and compute their own checks, Miller and Artie took a walk on the sunny side of the street.

Artie was not as talkative as usual, and, as Miller seldom did more than encourage a conversation once started, the two sauntered for several minutes in silence.

Then Artie spoke abruptly. "Miller," said he, "I got a hen on."

"What is it?"

"It's like this. Would you dally with politics if you thought you stood to win out a good thing?"

"That depends. *You're* not going into politics, are you?"

"They've got me entered, but I don't

E MAIN SQUEEZE

know whether I'll start or not. I'm
leary of it; I do n't mind tellin' you those."

" What do you mean ? "

" Well, mebbe you won 't understand.
I do n't like to feature myself, but in that
precinct where I hang out I'm purty
strong. I'm a good mixer and I've kind
o' got next to the live ones, and if I do
say it myself I think there's a lot of the
boys that 'd vote my way if I went after
'em hard. Do you know Jim Landon?"

" Who is he ? "

" He's the main squeeze in our ward,
or any way he used to be. He's one o'
the aldermen, and he's out for it again,
but good and scared that he can't win
out. He come to me last night at Hoover's
cigar store and give me a big talk. What
he wants is for me to come to the front for
him strong. He knows I've got a drag
in the precinct, and he says if I'll jump .
in and do what I can for him he'll see
that I got a good job in the town offices,

where I can cop out about twice what I 'm gettin' now.   Of course I 'm out for the long green — but I do n't know about this deal."

" Does he stand a good chance of being elected ? "

" That 's what keeps me guessin'. Two years ago he win in a walk, but this spring he had to do all kinds o' funny work to get the nomination.   There 's a lot o' people in the ward that 's got their hammers out and they 're knockin' him all they can.   They 'll put a crimp in him if things come their way."

" What 's the matter with him, anyway ? "

" Oh, they kind o' think he 's done too well.   Two years ago he was on his uppers and now he 's got money to burn. There 's some o' them guys out in our ward can 't make out how it is that Jimmy can afford to buy wine at four bucks a throw when he 's only gettin' three a week

out o' the job. They say they can't
stand for that kind o' work, and so there's
a lot o' them church people that boosted
him two years ago that's out now to skin
him. They've put up a new guy against
him and he's makin' a nasty fight."

"I don't understand yet what they've
got against your man."

"W'y, they're crazy at him. You see
two years ago he made the play that if
they put him in he was goin' down to the
city hall and change the whole works.
He was goin' to clean the streets and jack
up the coppers and build some more school-
houses. Jimmy says to 'em : ' Throw
things my way and I'll be the Johnny-
on-the-spot to see that everything's on the
level.' The talk was so good it went.
Well, you know what happened to Jimmy
when he got down there with them Indians
and begin to see easy money. He had n't
been in on the whack-up six weeks till he
was wearing one o' them bicycle lamps in

his neck-tie and puttin' in all his time at
the city hall waitin' for the easy marks to
come along and throw up their hands."

" I see.   He turned out to be a boodler, eh ? "

" I do n't see no way o' gettin' past it.
I like Jimmy.   He 's one o' them boys
that never has cold feet and there 's nothin'
too good for a friend, but, by gee, I guess
when it comes to doin' the nice, genteel
dip he belongs with the smoothest of 'em.
And he learned it so quick, too.   Ooh ! "

" Artie, that kind of a man is a thief
and that 's all you can make out of it,"
said Miller, with presbyterian severity.

" Mebbe that ain't no lie, neither.   He
would n't go out with a piece o' lead pipe
or do any o' that strong-arm work, but if
Jimmy saw a guy puttin' dough into
his pocket he would n't let on.   You
would n't have to feed him no knock-
out drops to make him take the coin, I
guess.   But the nerve o' the boy !   He

won 't never let on that he 's handled any
crooked money. When he was staked to
the office he did n't have a sou markee
except what was tied up in a bum little
grocery store. Now he 's got too strong
to tend store and his brother-in-law 's
runnin' it. He do n't do a thing in the
world except travel around with some more
o' them handy boys and lay for jack-pots.
And the talk he gives you ! Mamma !
He 's better 'n any o' them shell-workers
that used to graft out at the gover'ment
pier. W'y, he can set down and show you
dead easy that he done all that funny votin'
because it was a good thing for the workin'
boys. Sure ! That 's why he wants to stay
in, too — so as the tax-payers won 't get
the short end of it. On the square, if I
had his face I 'd start out sellin' them gold
bricks to Jaspers."

"You do n't mean to say that he has
any chance of being elected again ? "

"Oh, he 's got a chance all right. He 's

gone right down into his kick and dug up
the long green and he 's puttin' it out at
the booze joints. Some o' the saloons
he 's overlooked for a year or two, and
he 's got to make good with 'em to keep
'em from knockin'. But he 'll have the
whole push rootin' for him, and, then, of
course, there 's a lot more o' people say :
'Oh, well, Jim 's a good fellow and he 's been
white with me, and even if he does sand-
bag a few o' them rich blokies what 's the
diff?' I think he 's got a chance, all right.
I would n't like to start in and plug his
game and then find myself on a dead one."

"Artie, if you take my advice you 'll
keep out of it. What do you want with
a political job ?"

"Well, for one thing I want to get a
bank-roll as soon as I can and this place
he 's holdin' out pays good money."

"Yes, and even if you got it you 'd be
out again in a year or two and worse off
than ever. Besides, I would n't help

elect a man who sold his influence." Miller spoke with considerable feeling.

"As for that," resumed Artie, "you
need n't think I like Jim Landon's way
o' gettin' stuff. It 's just like this, though.
He 's gone out of his way two or three
times to do things for me and fixed me for
a pass to Milwaukee once, and, of course,
them things count. Everybody 's shakin'
him down this spring, and if he gets the
gaff he 'll be flat on his back. If I did n't
know him I 'd be against him hard. But
you do n't like to throw down a man that 's
treated you right, do you ?"

"I 've never been in politics, but I
should say that no young man could have
any excuse for voting for a boodler."

"Say, now listen. It comes election
day, see ? I go in the place and get in one
o' them little private rooms and I vote for
this stranger. Then I come out and meet
Jimmy. He puts out the hand and I go
and get a cigar with him and do the friend-

ship act. Would n't that be purty coarse work ?"

" It would n't be any worse than his promising to be honest and then turning out a boodler " said Miller.

" Well, I guess I 'll pass up the whole thing. Come to size it up, that ward 's goin' to be floatin' in beer the next two weeks, and I 'm not stuck on standin' around with them boys that smoke them hay-fever torches. For a man that do n't want to be a rounder, it 's too much like sportin' life. I did n't think you 'd O. K. the scheme. I 'll just tell Jimmy that I 'm out of it. That 's an awful wise move, too. I guess an easier way to get that roll 'd be to borrow a nice kit o' tools and go 'round blowin' safes."

CLAUDIE

XIII

"Where's he at?" asked the over-grown messenger boy, who had clumped slowly along the hallway and who now entered the room, leaving the door open behind him.

"Ain't he good?" asked Artie, turning to Miller, who was gazing at the messenger with a look of pained surprise in his eyes.

"Where's he at?" repeated the messenger boy.

He seemed rather large and old to be in the uniform, for there was a scrabble of soft beard on his chin. His face and hands appeared to have been treated with fine coal-dust, his cap leaned forward on one side of his head and whenever he spoke he had to make new disposition of a large amount of chewing tobacco which he carried in his mouth.

When he asked " Where 's he at ? " he pronounced it "where 'ce," and in all his subsequent talk he gave the " s " a soft and hissing sound well prolonged, to the evident enjoyment of Artie and the mild wonderment of Miller.

" Where 's who at ? " demanded Artie, adopting a frown and a harsh manner.

" W'y, t'e four-eyed nobs dat sent me out on t'e Sout' Side."

" Are you the same little boy ? Would n't that frost you, though, Miller ? This is little Bright-eyes that took the note for Hall."

" Aw, what 's eatin' you ? " asked the boy, giving a warlike curl to the corner of his mouth.

" Oh, ow ! listen to that. I 'll bet you 're the toughest boy that ever happened. What you been doin' all day —

playin' marbles for keeps or standin' in front o' one o' them dime museeums ? "

" Aw, say ; you t'ink you 're fly. Dat young feller sent me all t'e way to forty-t'ree ninety-t'ree Callamet av'noo. I could n't get back no sooner."

" Who was it the note was to ? "

" His rag, I guess."

"Oh-h-h-h ! His rag ! What do you think o' that, Miller ? Ain 't this boy a bird ! Can you beat him ? Can you *tie* him ? Boy, you 're all right."

" So are you — dat is, from y'r head up."

" An' the feet down, huh ? You 're one o' them ' Hully chee, Chonny,' boys, ain 't you ? You 're so tough they could n't dent you with an axe."

" Is dat so-o-o-o ? " asked the boy, with a frightful escape of " s " and a glare such as he must have used to terrify all the smaller boys at the call station.

"If I was as tough as you are I 'd be afraid o' myself, on the level."

" You t'ink you 're havin' sport wit' me, do n't you ? I seen a lot o' dem funny mugs before dis."

" W'y, Claudie, I would n't try to josh you. I think you 're a nice, clean boy. Ain 't you goin' to take off your gloves ? "

Miller leaned back in his chair and howled with laughter.

" I beg y'r pardon, Claudie," continued Artie. " I thought them was gloves you had on. Gee, is them your mits ? You 're a brunette, ain 't you ? "

The messenger boy had been somewhat taken back by the allusion to his " gloves," but he recovered and said, still gazing at Artie : " S-s-ay, you 're havin' all kinds o' fun wit' me, ain 't you ? Well, w'at you —anyt'ing you say cuts no ice wit' me."

" You 'd better smoke up or you 'll go out," suggested Artie. " You was a little slow on the come-back that last time. Get on to him, Miller ; he 's lookin' a hole in me."

" He has a bad eye," said Miller.

" Yes, and as the guy says on the stage, I do n't like his other one very well, neither. I 'll bet he 'd be a nasty boy in a fight. I 'd hate to run against him late at night. Them messenger boys is bad people. Guess what they train on."

" I do n't know," said Miller.

" Cocoanut pie. That ain't no fairy tale, neither. Cocoanut pie and milk, that 's what they live on. I 'll bet Claudie here with the face has got about three cocoanut pies wadded into him now. How about it, Claudie ? "

" Say," began the messenger boy, nodding his head slowly to emphasize his remarks, " I 'd give a t'ousand dollars if I had your gall."

" That 'll be all right. Keep the change. By the way, old chap, are you lookin' for any one ? "

This was another surprise for the boy.

ARTIE

" Yes-s-s, I 'm lookin' for some one,"
he replied.

" Who it is is it ? "

" W'y, t'e fellow dat wears de windows
in his face. I got a note here for him,"
and he pulled it out of his pocket.

" Looks like you 've been chewin' it.
That 's his desk over there. He got dead
tired o' waitin' for you and went out to
tell the police you was lost. I think
they 're draggin' the lake for you now."

" Aw, go ahead; dat 's right. Dere 's
lots o' you blokies t'ink you can have fun
wit' us kids."

" Get next to the walk, Miller; get on,
get on ! " exclaimed Artie, as the messenger boy moved over toward Hall's desk.
On the way he stopped for a moment and
spat copiously into a waste-basket.

" He walks like he had gravel in his
shoes, do n't he ? " said Artie. " Look at
the way he holds them shoulders. Ain 't
he tough, though ? "

118

"Some day you 'll get too gay an' a guy 'll give you a funny poke," remarked the messenger boy, as he slowly settled into young Mr. Hall's chair and again directed what was supposed to be a terrorizing stare at Artie.

"What did I tell you, Miller? Claudie 's a scrapper. He 'd just as soon give a guy a ' tump in de teet ' as look at him."

The boy gave a sniff of contempt and began an examination of the papers on Mr. Hall's desk, picking up some of the letters and studying them, his lips going through the motions of reading. Artie sat, with face illumined, and watched the boy. He was evidently fascinated by the display of supreme impudence.

"Ain't there nothin' we can do for you?" he asked. "Miller 's got some private letters you can read when you get through over there."

"Aw, go chase yourself," replied the boy.

" Well, Claudie, I 've seen a good many o' you boys, but you 're the best ever," remarked Artie. " If Hall 's tryin' to win out any South Side lady friend I do n't see as he could do better than send you out with the note. I think you 'll be liked wherever you go. Gee! you 've got that icehouse stare o' yours down pat. If you keep on springin' that you 'll scare somebody one o' these days."

"Aw, let go," said the boy in evident disgust. "When do I get to see t'e fellow dat sets here? Won't one o' youse pay me?"

" Miller, pay the boy and let him go. He ain 't had any cocoanut pie for nearly an hour now, have you, Willie — er — Claudie, I mean. What is your name, Claudie?"

" What 's it to you?"

"Nothin' much, only I wanted to know. You 've kind o' won me out. Here! Do n't move! I 'll bring the waste-basket over to you."

120

ARTIE

At that moment young Mr. Hall came in and said: " Ah, boy, have you that note for me?"

" S-s-s-ure. Where you been at? You 're helva duck to keep a kid waitin' here. You 've got 'o pay me ten cents more."

" Do n't be saucy," said young Mr. Hall, severely.

" Aw, rats!"

" You ain 't mad, are you, Claudie?" asked Artie, as the boy laboriously moved toward the door, making noises with his feet.

" Oh-h-h, but you t'ink you 're a kidder," replied the boy, with a sour smile.

" Look out! You 'll step on one o' your feet there in a minute."

Then they heard him go clump-clump-clump out through the hall and away.

" Confound such a boy!" exclaimed young Mr. Hall.

ARTIE

"Oh, he's all right," said Artie, "only you ain't used to his ways."

"He's tough enough," suggested Miller.

"Yes," said Artie, "I would n't be as tough as he thinks he is —not for a million dollars."

HE PRESIDENT

XIV

" Let 's walk out a little while and let
the wind blow on us," said Artie, when
the conversation had begun to lag.

He had found Mamie on the front stoop
with her father and mother. It was the
first warm night of the early spring, and
the tired people all along the street had
come into the open air, the older ones
to sit around the doorways and the chil-
dren to romp on the sidewalks.

Gas lamps are far apart in that street
and the houses are much alike — two
stories high, many of them having the
high stoop that leads steeply from the
sidewalk to the upper story. A stranger
might have had some trouble in finding
the Carroll house, but Artie knew the
neighborhood. He collided with the chil-

ARTIE

dren and said: "Do n't run me down,
kids." There was a carnation in his but-
tonhole and he clicked a walking-stick on
the uneven sidewalk. The smell of pipe
smoke, the balm of the cooler evening air
and the awakened cheerfulness of the
street, which he had never before seen so
lively, harmonized with his own feelings.
There was a spring song going in his heart,
and when he came to the Carroll stoop it
strove to find utterance in words.

"Ain 't this a James-dandy of a night?"
he asked, removing his hat. "I see all
you good people are takin' it in."

Mamie arose to greet him, and said
something in a low tone to her father.
Artie knew what it was.

"Stay where you are, Mr. Carroll,"
said he. "I 'll grab off a place here at
the end."

"Father was so warm he just took off
his coat and came out here to enjoy his
pipe," said Mamie, in way of explanation.

"I do n't blame him. Would n't you rather have a cigar, Mr. Carroll?"

"Well, I do n't mind. Have y' another?"

"Sure thing. You need n't be afraid o' that one. It 's got real tobacco in it. How are *you* to-night, Mrs. Carroll?"

"I 'm all right now, but this afternoon I thought I 'd keel over. Was n't it warm?"

"I should say yes."

Then there followed some more commonplace remarks about the weather, and at the first oppportunity Artie suggested taking a walk.

While Mamie was in the house putting on her hat Artie said: "You 've got lots o' kids up this way."

"The German family in the next house has nine," replied Mrs. Carroll. "If father could 'a' caught one o' them towheaded young 'uns this morning there 'd only been eight left. The boy built a bonfire right up against our fence."

"He could run too fast for me," said Mr. Carroll. "Oh, but he's a terror. We have some great youngsters around here. Do you want to get by me, Mamie? Look at the new hat on her."

Artie laughed and Mamie gave her father a playful slap on the arm.

"It's a hun," remarked Artie.

As he followed Mamie down the steps and away toward the corner he somehow felt, because of the silence behind, that Mr. and Mrs. Carroll were watching him and asking themselves whether he was what he pretended to be. On more than one occasion they had shown a liking for him. Certainly they had trusted him. He realized keenly, and for the first time, that they had been kind to him beyond anything he deserved, and with this realization came the resolve that he would never do anything to cause them to change their opinions.

"I'm afraid the old folks 'll think we're

givin' 'em the shake," said he, as Mamie slipped her arm within his.

" No, no. They do n't mind."

" I guess they 're wise enough to tumble to it that I do n't come rubberin' around this neighborhood every two or three nights just to see *them*."

Mamie laughed and put an added pressure on his arm. The gas-lights leaped into balls of flame and Artie felt himself rising into the air. What more could he ask? And yet, as they passed the corner, he was beaming foolishly and had lost his voice.

He had something to tell Mamie — something which would be significant; something to warn her of the supreme question and prepare her for it.

They had come into the business street, where the trolley cars ran and the light was plentiful.

" A little more weather like this and we 'll be hittin' the park," he observed.

" I 'll be glad," she replied.

They walked in silence for few moments and then he said: " Mame, I 've got some good news."

" For me ? "

" Well, I s'pose — you may be glad to hear it."

" What is it ? "

" I got a boost in my pay."

" Oh, that 's lovely."

" I 'm gettin' twenty a week now."

" Now I 'm Jealous. All I get is eight."

" Say, Mame, I 'm sore to see you workin' at all."

" I had to do something when I got out of school, and they did n't need me around the house. I would n't mind it if I had a nicer man to work for."

" Who is the main guy up at your place — the pie-face I spoke to the day I come up to see you ? "

" Yes, that 's him."

" I got it in good and hard for them fel-

lows. Do you know, Mame, this town's full
of a lot o' two-by-four dubs that 's got into
purty fair jobs and it 's made 'em so swelled
up that you want to take a crack at one of
'em the minute you see him. I 'll bet
that guy up in your place do n't know
nothin' on earth except how to hold down
his measly job, and he got that doin' all
the mean work around the place. It does
me lots o' good to call one o' them proud
boys down. If I ever go up there again
and he makes any funny play at me I 'll
come back at him so strong that he won 't
know what landed on him. Them fellows
is counterfeits. They have to put on a
horrible front so as to cover up what they
do n't know. I never see one o' them
fellows yet that was n't a four-flush.
Take a guy that bellers at kids and bluffs
women and put him up against a man of
his own weight and he 's a cur. If I ever
put up my hands against that fellow he 'd
run clear to the roof to get away."

ARTIE

Mame laughed and said: " You 've got him sized up just right."

" I 'm workin' for a square fellow," continued Artie. " He 's *all* right. I used to give him all kinds o' hot and cold roasts, but since he went to the front for me and got my salary whooped I 've got to be with him. I 'll tell you, Mame, he 's this kind. If you 'd go up to Morton to-morrow and say: ' How about it; can you take hold and run the earth for a year?' he 'd put on one o' them dead easy smiles and say he could do it without turnin' a hair. He 's got the nerve to tackle anything. He do n't know nothin', but he do n't need to as long as he can make suckers think he 's all right. There 's Miller I 've told you so much about. He knows more about the business than Morton ever wanted to know, but Morton draws more stuff just because Miller ain 't got the face. So I 've got wise to this fact: No matter

what you 've got in your hand play it as if
you had a royal flush for a bosom hold-
out. I weaken on no proposition. If they
wanted me to be president o' the whole
shootin' match, I 'd jump in, grow some
side-whiskers and put up as tall a con
game as that old stiff we 've got down
there now. His office hours is from 11:00
to 11:30 .and he ain't nothin' but a ham-
rester when he *is* there."

Artie had become warmed up, and was
walking fast. They stopped at a corner
to allow a drove of bicyclers to pass by,
and Artie saw the red globes of a drug-
store across the street.

"Let 's have some o' the cold stuff,
Mame," said he, and he led her over to
the place.

"Give the lady some strawberry because it 's red," said he to the clerk.

" No, you 'll not," said she. " I want
chocolate ice cream."

" Well, professor, you can make mine the same. Be a good fellow, too, when it comes to droppin' in the ice cream."

" Oh, we put in good measure," said the red-headed boy, as he dug into the freezer.

" That's right. I think you'll do a nice little business on this corner."

ILLER

XV

" I do n't know about this, Artie," said Miller, as they alighted from the trolley car. "I have no business coming out here with you."

"There you go again!" exclaimed Artie. "Ain't I told you that anybody I bring stands ace-high? W'y, I 've been toutin' you to Mame till she 's dead crazy to see you. Do n't go to weak'nin' on me at this stage o' the game. You 're just as welcome there as you are in the street."

" I dare say," replied Miller, with a nervous little laugh, " but I think you 'll have to do most of the talking."

" Let go of that, too. You won 't get no frozen face at this place that I 'm steerin' you against. Just cut loose the same as if you was at home. I guess you ain 't goin' to find no cracked ice in the chairs, and, as I 've told you time and again, this girl ain 't stuck on frills. She comes purty near bein' able to size up a guy for what he 's worth, and you and her 'll get along all right."

Notwithstanding these hopeful assurances, Miller was decidedly nervous as they approached the Carroll house. It was only after much persuasion on the part of Artie that he had been induced to come along and now that they were so near the place his apprehensions grew. Miller knew a great deal, but he had never learned how to keep down his pulse and temperature when he was in the presence of a young woman.

"Remember," said Artie, as he preceded Miller up the steps. " Do n't be leary about cuttin' in. Just play you owned the house."

Mamie opened the door and said : " Hello, there," and then, when she saw that Artie was not alone, she gave a small and startled " Oh ! "

" Peel your coat and put it any old place," said Artie to Miller.

" Why, Artie," said she, reprovingly.

They were detained in the hallway for a few moments. Artie felt that perhaps he should have presented Miller at the moment of entering, but he preferred to wait until they reached the front room, where there was a full sweep of space at his command.

The critical moment having arrived, Mamie having retreated until she stood beneath the chandelier and Miller having come in from the hall and placed himself, stolid and upright, beside one of the plush chairs, Artie said : " Mame, I want you to shake hands with my friend Mr. Miller, the best ever. Miller, this is little Mame, the girl that makes 'em open all the windows to look at her when she goes along the street."

"I'm so glad to meet you, Mr. Miller," said Mamie. "I've heard so much about you."

She extended her hand and as Miller grasped it and mumbled something, Artie very facetiously remarked, "Take your corners."

Now, if this was his plan for causing Miller to feel perfectly at home, it was not an entire success. Miller laughed rather awkwardly and backed into a chair, where he sat and smiled in a fixed and helpless condition until Mamie came to his rescue.

"I suppose you've learned by this time that you mustn't pay any attention to what Artie says," she began. "He doesn't mean half he says."

"Here! How about this?" interrupted Artie. "You ain't goin' to begin knockin' the first thing. Pay no attention to what she says about me, Miller. Just copper it. I think she's got her roastin' clothes on to-night."

"I'm afraid I'll have to believe a good many things that he has told me about you," said Miller, with an effort.

"What has he been telling you?"

"Slow up there a little. Be careful," said Artie.

"He said a great many complimentary things about you," persisted Miller.

"Who, me?" demanded Artie. "What are you tryin' to do — string the poor girl? All I ever told you about Mame was the time she shook me for that Indian. I'll tell you about her, Miller. I'm good old car-fare and show-tickets when there's nobody playin' against me, but as soon as any other guy gets in the game she puts me off on the sub bench. I ain't in the play at all. You're here to-night. Am I in it? Well, I should say nit."

Miller laughed good-naturedly and Mamie passed off into an attack of giggles from which she could not easily recover.

"You don't expect me to pay much

attention to you when there's any one else around, do you?" she asked with the merest suggestion of a wink at Miller.

"Certainly not. I'm supposed to be playin' a thinkin' part to-night. I ain't really in the cast at all. I think I come on with a spear in the third act."

"You've heard him talk like that before, have n't you?" asked Mamie of Miller.

"Oh, yes; I've become accustomed to it."

"Oh, what a swipe?" exclaimed Artie. "I think I'll have to lay quiet for awhile after that. What are you doin', Miller; turnin' against me—takin' her part?"

"My goodness, Artie, what did he say that was n't all right?" asked Mamie.

"There you are, Miller. She's huntin' a scrap because I spoke cross to you. I told you I would n't be in it after I brought you up here."

"Artie, I want you to behave. I'm

going to ask Mr. Miller all about how you carry on at the office."

" Oh, his conduct is very good," Miller hastened to say.

" That's what you boys always say about each other. Does he ever work?"

" Do I ever work!" Artie interrupted. " Do you think I could travel on my shape? She ought to see us doin' the slave act there the first of every month; eh, Miller?"

" We have to work hard enough," said Miller.

" He's told me all this," said Mamie; "but he 'kids' so much, as he calls it, that I do n't know when he's telling the truth and when he is n't. Why, do you know, Mr. Miller, the first time I met him, he told me his name was something-or-other and that he was on the Board of Trade — oh, the worst string of stuff you ever heard."

Miller had to laugh, because he had

already been told the whole story by Artie.

" Did you believe it ? " he asked.

" Believe it ? I should say not. He told me the worst whoppers you ever heard about how much money he made and lost on the Board of Trade. What's more, just to show you the cheek of that boy, the fellow that he had come over and introduce him I never saw before in all my life."

Miller had to laugh in earnest. Artie had told him the same story, but had claimed that Mamie believed everything she heard.

For once Artie was red, embarrassed and at a loss to reply. He smiled feebly when Miller laughed, and then he managed to say: " I guess you faked up some purty good fairy yarns yourself that night."

" I was trying to keep up with you," said Mamie, gaily.

ARTIE

Artie's grin widened and he glanced significantly at Miller.

"What did I tell you?" he asked. "Ain't she a child wonder?"

And by that time Miller was well enough acquainted to join in and talk on many topics.

It was after ten o'clock when they left the house and started for the car.

"Well, will she do?" asked Artie almost as soon as the door had closed behind them.

"Yes, indeed," replied Miller, warmly. "She's an awfully nice girl."

"Nothin' mushy, eh? None o' this soft work?"

"No, sir. She's a good, sensible girl."

"How about her bein' a good looker?"

"Artie, you may think I'm trying to flatter you, but really she is a very pretty girl — very pretty."

"Say, I tumbled that she was the real stuff the first time I ever see her. You

141

got next to how she give me that horrible jolt about the dance, did n't you ? "

" I should say so."

" Now, there 's a wise girl. She knew awful well that I 'd told you about meetin' her at the dance, and how I caught her that night, and she just brought the thing up to square herself with you. She did n't want you to think that any Reub could go up and flag her."

" Oh, well, you can see that she is n't that kind of a girl."

" Sure. They do n't grow 'em on the Lake Shore drive any better-behaved than she is now."

UNG MR. HALL

XVI

Every breeze that came in at the open windows was as soft as velvet. The warm sunshine had tempered it until the last sting of winter was gone.

Miller and Artie had removed their coats and unbuttoned their vests. They worked listlessly, and occasionally one of them would lean back and gaze sleepily out at the walls and roofs and the distant ribbon of lake, now dotted here and there with moving specks.

" A man ought to be pinched for workin' a day like this," Artie finally observed.

" Is n't it delightful?" said Miller. " This is the time of year when a man feels like getting out into the country."

" That ain't no lie, neither. You do n't

see very many Johnny-jump-ups growin'
along Dearborn street, do you ? "

" Do you expect to get away from
town often this summer ? "

" Gee, I can't go very far. Since I 've
started plantin' my stuff in the bank and
plunkin' in a few cases every month on the
buildin' and loan game, I 've got to play
purty close to my bosom, I 'll tell you
those. Night before last, though, I was
fixin' it up with Mame to take a little run
over to St. Joe or up to Milwaukee on the
boat. When they let you ride all day on
the boat for a dollar a throw; w'y, that 's
where I cut in freely. But they do n't
get my game at any o' them summer re-
sorts where they set you back five big
elegant bucks a day for a room about as
big as that telephone box over there. Then
if you want anything to chew you 've got
to square the waiter every time you go in
the dinin'-room. I went up against one
o' them places last summer. I com-

menced owin' money to that hotel before I got off the train. They cleaned me in two days, but then, as they say down on State street, I was n't very dirty when I landed."

" If I 'm going to take a vacation," said Miller, " I 'd rather get right out into the country. Do n't you like the country ? "

" Well, I ain't dead sure about that. I 'spose the country's all right to a man that 's lived there, but you take some wise boy that was brought up in town, and you throw him out on a farm, and he's the worst ever. You 've seen them boys around the Union station comin' in with their red-topped boots and high hats and paper grips — well, when you see them fallin' into coal-holes and bein' snaked out by fake hotel-runners you think they 're purty new, do n't you ? Well, say, there ain't one o' them that 's half the horrible mark that some Chicago dub is when he goes up against that farm game. If he

do n't look like a yellow clarinet in twenty-
four hours you can mark me down for a
sucker. They can 't spring none o' that
happy-childhood-days-down-on-the-farm
business on me. I 've been next, I 'll tell
you those."

" I did n't know that you were ever on
a farm," said Miller, laughing.

" I was there once, all right, and I got it
throwed into me so hard I was good and
sore, too. Four years ago this summer
— that was before my father died — my
uncle Matt, that 's got a farm a little ways
from Galesburg, wrote for me to come
down and visit 'em. The old gentleman
asked me if I wanted to go, and I said,
' Sure thing; in a minute.' I 'd been
readin' them con story-books about pickin'
flowers and goin' fishin' and dubbin' around
the woods out in the country, and I thinks
to myself : ' This is a cinch. I 'll go down
there and dazzle them jays.' So I went
down there, and a cousin o' mine, Spencer

ARTIE

Blanchard, met me at the train with a
buggy and drove me out. I got there in
time for supper, and they all give me the
glad hand and jollied me up, and I kind o'
thought that first night that I 'd be a warm
proposition out there. Well, holy smoke!
about the time they got the dishes washed
up the uncle says to me, ' I guess we 'd
better turn in.' ' What do you mean ? ' I
says ; ' go to bed ?' ' Sure thing,' says he.
' We got to get all kinds of an early start
in the morning.' I could n't stand for that.
I put up a holler right at the jump. I told
'em I was just usually beginnin' to enjoy
myself about nine o'clock in the evening.
They said I could set up if I wanted to,
and then they ducked and turned in. Well,
I did n't want to turn in, but there was
nothin' to keep me up. I set out by the
pump for a little while smokin' and listenin'
to them katydids gettin' in their work, and
then I went in the house and went to bed,
but I could n't get to sleep before mid-

night. It seemed to me I 'd been poundin'
my ear about ten minutes when somebody
walloped me in the back and hollered,
' Get up.' Well, I set up in bed, and —
honest, Miller, this ain't no kid — it was
dark outside. ' What's the trouble ? ' I
says. ' Is the house on fire ? ' It was
my cousin Spencer that give me the jolt
in the back. ' It's time to get up,' he
says. I asked him what time it was, and
what do you think he said ? This is on
the level, too. He says, ' It's past
four.' When he said that I did n't know
what kind of a combination I 'd struck."

" I guess people in the country often get
up that early in the summer time, especially in the busy season," said Miller.

" They 'd never got me up, I tell you
those, only that fresh cousin o' mine
grabbed me by the leg and pulled me out.
Oh, he's a playful guy, all right. Well,
I put on my clothes and went downstairs,
dead on my feet. You see, I was shy four

or five hours' sleep. When they see me they all give me the horse-laugh, even the hired girl. My aunt asked me what time I got up when I was in town, and I said never before seven o'clock, and then they all yelled again. They seemed to think I was wrong in my nut out there. Everything I done or said they give me the ha-ha."

" Of course life in the city is much different," said Miller.

" Well, I guess yes. I know this town like a book. I can begin at the first card and go through the deck, but out there — they lose me. They had me lookin' like a Reub all the time. The worst one was the hired hand. His name was Elias. I see him up here the time of the World's Fair, dodgin' cable cars and lookin' up at the skyscrapers. He was dead lucky to get out o' town without havin' his clothes lifted, and, at that, I ain't sure he did. But down at the farm, he was the wise guy and I was the soft mark. What do you think? The second day I was there I goes out in the field where they was cuttin' down the oats with one o' them bindin' machines, and 'Lias asked me to go back to the barn and ask Uncle Matt if he had a left-handed monkey wrench. How was I to know? I ain't up on monkey-wrenches. Gee, I went drillin' way back to the barn through the hot sun, and when I sprung the left-handed monkey-wrench on the uncle it made a horrible hit with him. He hollered around till I got kind o' sore. Then he went in the house and told them and they all had a fit about it. But you ought o' seen 'Lias when he come in at night. He was all swelled up over the way he throwed it into me. He thought he was a better comedian than Nat Goodwin. He must a' gone for two miles all around tellin' that monkey-wrench story, and a lot o' the hands used to come over and kid me. They'd laugh and slap their legs and say, ' By Jing !' They had me crazy. I used to think it was n't on the square to josh a man because he was from the country, but do n't you fool your-self — them country people won 't do a thing to a city guy if they ever get him out where they can take a good, fair crack at him."

" It was all in fun, though, was n't it ?" asked Miller.

" Oh, sure ; they thought they was givin' me a good time. There was a kid cousin o' mine, Rutherford Hayes Blanch-ard — would n't that name frost you ? — that jollied me into ridin' bareback on one o' the old pelters they had around the place. I was up in the air most o' the time, and after I got through ridin' mebbe you think I was n't sore. This same kid took me down to the crick to go swim-min'. I burned the skin off o' my back, got a peach of a stone bruise on my foot, and while I was in, 'Lias and Spencer come

over and tied my clothes in hard knots.
That's just a sample. Oh, I had a nice
time. After a day or two I shook my
town clothes and made up for a farmer
but I couldn't play the part. They used
to make me try to hitch up the team without anyone helpin', and then they'd all
stand around and kid me me when I made
bad breaks. It was a cinch that I'd fall
down. I didn't know a whiffle-tree from
a tug. Then they had me milkin', too. I
don't know whether you're on to it or
not, but if you try to play up to a cow on
the wrong side of her she's liable to make
a sassy pass and land the knockout.
Well, the first night they took me out to
milk they steered me up against the bum
side o' the cow. I'm purty game myself,
an' I didn't want to quit, but she was too
good for me. She kept me busy for about
five minutes,and then I went to my corner
and said I had enough. Say, the whole
push had been leanin' on the fence laughin'

at me till they cried. I guess they had
more fun around that place while I was
there than they ever had before. I stood
it for about ten days, helpin' 'em work in
the fields, gettin' all tanned up and roundin'
in to supper every night smellin' like a
laundry, and then I kind o' figured it out
that farm life was too swift for me. I
kind o' wanted to see the 'lectric lights
and the tall houses again. So I said I was
goin'. They made an awful kick for me
to stay. They knew they had a good
thing. But I broke away."

"Then you're not fond of the country?"

"It's this way. I would n't mind goin'
out for awhile if I could play myself off as
company, but when it comes to bein' one
of the family — nit, nit."

XVII

"Well, I'm goin' to be one o' them boys," said Artie, after he had seated himself and turned half-way around so that he could see Miller.

"What boys?" asked Miller.

"Them bike people with the fried-egg caps and the wall-paper stockins'. I'm goin' to be the sassiest club boy in the whole push. You just wait. In about a week I'll come hot-footin' in here with my knee-pants and a dinky coat, and do the club yell."

"I knew you'd get it sooner or later."

"This thing got the half-Nelson on me before I know it. One night I goes to bed feelin' all right and the next mornin' when I woke up I was wrong. There

BIKE PEOPLE

was somethin' ailed me, but I was n't wise to it. The first thing I know I was stoppin' along the street lookin' at the wheels in the windows and gettin' next to the new kinds o' saddles and rubber-neckin' to read the names on the tires, and all that business. Then I begin to see that I had it the same as everybody else."

" I noticed that you 'd been talking bicycle lately, but I did n't know you were going to get one."

" I 'll tell you. I had a spiel with Mame last night and we fixed it up that if we did n't ride wheels this summer we would n't be in it at all, so I 'm goin' to do the sucker act and blow myself."

" Does Mamie ride ?"

" Does she? She 's a scorchalorum. You ought o' seen her pushin' around the block last night on the Connelly girl's wheel. I told her if she ever went through the park speedin' like that she 'd have all the sparrow cops layin' for her."

of 'em. I could n't stand for nothin' like
that. They was out just to make a show
o' themselves. This year it 's different.
Everybody 's gone nutty on the proposition. You can go out on a bike now
without every driver tryin' to upset you
and all the people joshin' you about your
knee-pants."

" It 's wonderful, the number of people
riding wheels this spring," said Miller.

" I 'll tell you they 've gone daffy and
I 'm one of 'em. I 'm goin' to be the
worst fan in the whole bunch. What do
you think last Sunday out ·at Lincoln
Park ? Old geezers — ye-e-s, the white-
haired boys that you 'd think was too stiff
to back a wheel out of a shed, they was
out there in them dizzy togs cuttin' up
and down the track like two-year-olds.
And old girls, too — girls from away back,
about the crop o' '45 — fat ones, too —
poundin' the pedals and duckin' in and out
past the rigs ! W'y, when I see it I put

ARTIE

both hands in the air and I says : 'Well, when the old people can cut in on this game it 's about time for me to begin to associate.' I 'll be with 'em, too, next Sunday."

"Are you going to wear a suit ? " asked Miller.

" Well, I'm a little leary on that. I do n't want to get too gay on the jump. Mame wants me to get one and be right in line with all them club boys, but when she first sprung it on me I said : 'Nix; if I ever come up here with one o' them funny suits on the old man might take a shot at me.' Here's a funny thing about that. Here 's somethin' that 'll knock you cold. Last night when I gets to the house to see the girl, Mrs. Carroll's on the front porch and I could see she was hot about something. I asked her if anything had gone wrong and she says, 'Mr. Blanchard, there 's an old man around the corner makin' a fool of himself. If you 've

got any drag with him I wish you 'd go
and get him in the house before he breaks
his neck.' I was n't on to what she was
talkin' about, but she pointed to the
corner and I walked over there and say —
this is a good thing—if there was n't Mame's
old man takin' a fall out of a wheel. He'd
borrowed it from one o' the neighbors, and
this guy was holdin' him on and jollyin'
him along. 'Do n't be afraid,' he says,
'you won't fall.' The old man's eyes
was hangin' out, and he was workin' them
handle-bars like a man twistin' a brake.
Gee, he was a sight. I had to holler and
then he looked up and saw me. Course
that rattled him and over he went. He
made a fair fall, too, both shoulders on
the ground and Mr. Bike on top of him.
You ought o' heard some o' the large blue
language the old man got rid of soon as
we took the wheel off of him. I did n't
know it was in him. 'Try it again,' this
neighbor says, and he was takin' long

ARTIE

chances on gettin' his wheel smashed at
that. But the old man would n't listen to
it. He went limpin' back to the house,
and Mrs. Carroll says : ' Well, I hope
you 're satisfied now.' The old man give
her the cold eye, and then he says to me :
' She 'd talk that way if I 'd been killed.'
I guess Mame's mother is the only people
on the North Side that ain't monkeyin'
with a wheel."

" When do you and Mamie make your
first appearance ? "

"As soon as we can get the wheels. If
I do n't get mine inside of a week I'll go
bug-house. I'm dreamin' wheels, I tell
you. Last night I dreamt I was goin'
along at about forty miles an hour and run
into a steam roller."

" Did it break the wheel ? "

" I give it up. I woke up and found
myself tryin' to get the strangle hold on
the pillow."

" Is Mamie going to wear bloomers ? "

"Is she? Is she goin' to wear 'em —
bloomers? Not on your facial expression.
The first time we talked wheel I got up
and declared myself on the bloomer business. I done the tall talk. I told her
any time she sprung them Turkish village
clothes on her Artie boy, all bets was goin'
to be declared off."

"Why, what's the matter? Bloomers
are all right."

"They 're all right on some other guy's
girl, but they do n't go in my set. When
I see my girl come on a wheel I want to
know whether it 's her or some Board o'
Trade clerk. I do n't want to be kept
guessin'. "

"Why, what 's wrong with bloomers?"

"I 'll tell you. The first one I ever see
in bloomers was a lemon-faced fairy that
ought o' been picked along about cen-
tennial year. She come peltin' along

ARTIE

Michigan avenue with one o' them ballet-
girl smiles splittin' that face o' hers, and
I aint kiddin' when I tell you that a
horse jumped up on the sidewalk and tried
to get in the Risholoo hotel so as to pass
it up.   For a month afterwards I 'd see
that face at night and I 'd wake up and
holler : ' Take it away ! '   From the minute I see this good thing on Michigan I 'm
dead sore on all bloomers.   I never see a
good-lookin' girl wear 'em yet.   Some of
'em might have been good lookers before
they got into 'em, but after that—nit.
You need n't be afraid o' Mame, and
what 's more, I do n't want to talk about
her wearin' them things at all.   I like her
too well.   Do you think I 'm goin' out
ridin' with her and have a lot o' cheap
skates stoppin' to play horse with her
everywhere we go ?   Not in a thousand
years.   Besides, she do n't have to make
up like a man to make people look at her.

She ain't like some o' the others. W'y, she kills 'em dead in her street clothes. Bloomers! Well, if Mame goes with me she goes as a girl, and that ain't no lie, neither."

UPPERS

quired Artie. " I s 'pose he did. He 's
on to the story of my past life."

" No," said Miller. " I was just telling him that if he wanted to know anything about Chicago you were the man
that could tell him."

" Well, that 's a good send off. What
are you doin' ? Passin' me off as one o'
the sights o' the town ? I s 'pose you
told him that every visitor to Chicago
ought to see Lincoln Park, the stock-
yards, the sky-scrapers and Artie Blanchard and then buy a box o' candy for the
loved ones at home."

" No, but I told him you were just as
good as a guide-book."

" Better. I can put him next to things
that ain't in the guide-books. Come over
here next to the window where there 's a
draught, Mr. Miller. You might as well
take the air freely. That 's the only thing
in Chicago that you 'll get for nothin'."

" I believe you 're about right," remarked the cousin, as he moved over to a place near the window. "Coming up the street this morning I wanted a glass of water, and I finally had to go into a saloon and buy it."

" If you 'd had a beer thirst you 'd have been all right. Is this the first time you 've been up against the town ? "

" No, I was here a week the time of the World 's Fair, but I did n't get into this part of town much."

" Well, what do you think of it as far as you 've got ? Warm town, eh ? "

" Yes, indeed ; wonderful. I always feel rather lost when I get in the crowds."

" I s 'pose it is that way for a day or two, but you 'd soon get used to it."

" I do n't believe I would. There are too many people here. I 'm afraid I 'd never get along in Chicago."

" You want to get over that in a hurry. Of course there 's an awful push in the streets here any day, and I s 'pose when you

ARTIE

first get in you kind o' feel that you 're up
against a lot o' wise city mugs and that
they must be purty fly because they live
right here in town. I 've had people tell
me that 's the way they felt at first, but it
did n't take 'em long to find out there 's
just as many pin-heads on State street as
you 'll find anywhere out in the woods."

"Oh, I suppose a man would learn
about the city in a little while?"

"Cert. It ain't where a man 's born or
where he was raised that puts him in any
class. It 's whether he 's got anything
under his hat. I seen too many o' these
boys kind o' jump in from the country and
make a lot o' city boys look like rabbits.
You see, Mr. Miller, when a guy comes in
from the country he figures it out : 'Here,
I 'm goin' against a tough proposition, and
I 've got to hump myself to keep up.'
He 's willin' to learn a few things and do
the best he can. If he feels that way
he stands to win out. But if he comes

canterin' into town to be a dead-game sport and set a pace for all the boys, w'y, he do n't last. It's a small town, but it's too big for any one boy to come in from the country and scare it. Them sporty boys do n't last. They get in with a lot o' cheap skates and chase around at nights and think they 're the real thing, and then in a couple o' moons they go back home and leave all their stuff in hock. They think they 're fly, but they ain't."

"I know some that have done that very thing."

"Sure you do. I ain 't roastin' no man 'cause he 's from the country. You go along Prairie avenue and see all o' them swell joints where the fat boys with side-whiskers hang out. Well, them boys all come in from the country, but they had sense enough to saw wood and plant a little coin when it begin to come easy. I 'm tellin' you, the worst suckers you 'll find is some o' these city people that know it all to begin with. They got such a long start on everybody else that they do n't need to learn nothin'. If they know the names o' the streets, what shows is in town next week, what color of a necktie to flash and what was the score at the ball game they think they come purt' near bein' dead wise. You live here in town awhile and you 'll get on to them people. Say! I know a lot o' boys that 's got just enough sense to put in workin' hours and then go ridin' a wheel. You could n't set 'em down and tell 'em a thing. Any of 'em that 's got himself staked to a spring suit and knows the chorus o' 'Paradise Alley' thinks he 's up to the limit. You can make book that them boys 'll be workin' on bum salaries when they 're gray headed, and what 's more, they 'll be workin' for some Reub that come into town wearin' hand-me-downs."

" Well, I suppose folks out in the

country do give the city people too much credit for being smart," said the visitor.

"Oh, we 've got 'em smart enough, all right, all right, but I 'm tellin' you about the cheap ones. You 're a stranger here and you see some guy goin' along State street puttin' on a horrible front, tryin' to kill women right and left, a big piece o' rock salt on his necktie, and you say, 'Hully gee, I wonder who that case o' swell is; Marshall Field or P. D. Armour ?' Well, say, it 's a ten to one shot that all that that fellow 's got in the world he 's got right with him, and at that it ain't no cinch he 's wearin' underclothes. You 've got to learn these things. You don 't know — mebbe that guy can 't spell through the first reader. Any old farmer with one o' them bunches on his chin could buy up him and a hundred more like him. Well, he 's just the kind of a counterfeit that 'd go out in the country and play himself off

as the real boy because he lives in the city.
Now, don't you fool yourself for a minute,
Mr. Miller. Take my tip. We've got
just as many suckers up here as you've
got down your way."

"I think you're right about that," said
Miller, who had been listening.

"You know it. Take them mashers
along State street. Can you beat 'em anywhere ? Then a little farther south you'll
see them stranded boys, goin' around on
their uppers and takin' a dip at the free
lunch when nobody's lookin'. They'd
sooner stand around in town and starve to
death than get out somewhere and make a
stand for the coin. Any one o' them vags
thinks he's too good to go out in the
country or to some little town and live
decent."

"It's tough down that way. I walked
up through there this morning," said the
visiting Miller.

"You can get any kind of a game you

want down there, but you 're safe if you
do n't go huntin' trouble. Any man that
keeps hot-footin' right along and says
nothin' to nobody is all right. Of course,
when one of these new boys comes in and
raps on the bar and says he 's got money
to burn there 's always some handy man
right there to give him a match. When
that kind of a mark comes in they get
out the bottle o' knock-out drops and get
ready to do business. A man like you,
Mr. Miller, won't have no trouble here.
And for goodness sake do n't think you 're
up against anything great when you 're
minglin' with Chicago people. When
you come to know the town it 's as common as plowed ground. I know a good
show I 'll take you to to-night."

XIX

It was Saturday morning and Artie came in wearing his bicycle clothes.

"How do you like 'em?" he asked, turning about so that Miller and young Mr. Hall could see the hang of the coat. "Reduced from nineteen bones to seven seventy-five. Are you next to the stockin's? I guess I ain't got no shape or nothin'."

"It looks first rate on you," said young Mr. Hall.

"Well, why not, why not? I think I'm one o' the purtiest boys that works here in the office — anyway, that's what a good many people tell me."

"You did n't have it made, did you?" asked Miller.

RENT

good — I'll take you out some night and let you meet some o' the real folks."

"Oh, thanks," said young Mr. Hall, with a little twitch, suggestive of sarcasm, at one corner of his mouth. "Do you think you could introduce me to society."

"I could take you where you'd have to shake that Miss Maud business and comb your hair different or else go to the wall. If you ever went out to the Carrolls and sprung that gum-drop talk the old man wouldn't do a thing to you."

"It must be a pleasant sort of place," said young Mr. Hall, who had flushed up at the reference to the "Miss Maud business."

"The best ever—if you belong."

Young Mr. Hall smiled complacently and said: "Now I know why you've changed so much lately. I kind of believed you were still stuck on the girl."

"Who's changed? What are you talkin' about?"

" Why, you have. I 've noticed you never chew tobacco any more for one thing. Did she make you stop ? "

" No, she did n't. Well, you 've got a rind, ain't you ? What if she had ? What 's it to you ? "

" Nothing, only I can notice the change. You do n't cuss like you used to, nor smoke as much, and I 've seen you writing letters on that square paper and looking out of the window with the funniest kind of a look —— "

" Break away ! Say, I believe you 're tryin' to kid me. You talk like a man that was full of dope."

" I 'll leave it to Miller," persisted young Mr. Hall. " Has n't he changed, Miller ? Gracious me, I could notice it. I didn't know what the reason was, because after that first time he never told me anything about this."

" Oh, get tired, can't you ! " interrupted

Artie. " You must think you 're good if you can string me."

"I 'll leave it to Miller," repeated young Mr. Hall.

" Well," said Miller, laughing, " of course Artie has changed some, but——"

" There ! " exclaimed young Mr. Hall, triumphantly.

" Humph ! " said Artie. His face was red and he was certainly flustered. " It 'd be a dead lucky thing if some more people around the shop 'd change a little. They could n't be any punker 'n they are now."

But young Mr. Hall did not retort. He had made his point and was satisfied.

A few moments later young Mr. Hall put on his hat and started away on his daily round of collections. Artie turned from his desk and said to Miller : " Say, that boy kind o' had me down on the mat, did n't he ?"

" Do n't mind what he says."

" Yes, but he had the best of it. I

did n't s'pose he 'd noticed I was goin'
queer. They say a man never does know
it when he goes off the jump. On the
level, though, he 's dead right. I ain't like
I was the first time I met the girl. No
more chasin' around at nights, no blowin'
my stuff against a lot o' dubs and no more
boozin'."

" I 'd noticed that."

" Sure. I ain't had a package since that
night I told you about, and then they made
me take it."

" Package ? What 's that ? "

" W'y, a load, a jag! Smoke up!
Do n't go out on me. You ought to
know what a package is."

" I never had one."

" Well, I 've had 'em when I had to
lay down in the grass and hold on with
both hands to keep from fallin' off the
earth. I 've had 'em when I made tracks
like a man drivin' geese. I was like lots
more o' them sporty boys — wanted to

throw in the big bowls just to show I was nice people. There ain't a thing in it. Most o' them West Side boys I started in to train with got to be dead tough. I do n't want to star myself, but I think I had enough wiseness to switch. I ain't no blue-ribbon boy, but if you ever see little old Artie with a load o' peaches you can just take him and drop him in the river and say : ' Here goes nothin'.' "

" There 's nothing like a good, sensible girl to straighten a fellow up."

" Mebbe that ain't no lie, neither. She ain't never struck me to do nothin', but I just says : ' Here, you big mark, if you 're goin' to be around with a nice girl, why, you 've got to be nice people.' If there 's anything that makes me sore it 's to see some swell-lookin' girl goin' along with a guy actin' like a Reub or a dead tough. If he done his best, you know, he could n't belong with her. If I do say it myself, I 've used Mame the best I know how and

been purty square. Of course a man livin'
in this Indian village may think he's on
the square as long as he keeps out o' the
cooler, but I know I ain't been as tough as
a lot more. What knocks me is to think
this mamma's boy got on to me. I must
be gettin' purty far along when that guy
gets next and tries to play horse with me.
Everybody must be on. I s'pose them ele-
vator boys is sayin': 'Well, about day
after to-morrow they'll put his nobs into
cell 13 and send for the doctors.'"

"Nonsense, nonsense," said Miller,
laughing in spite of himself. "You're all
right. I wish I was stuck on some girl.
Then I'd know what to do evenings."

"Evenings! Say, Miller, there ought
to be about ten evenings every week. If
things keep on the way they've been since
both of us went daffy on the bike game,
I'll have to give up my job here and move
Mr. Trunk up to the Carroll joint. I'm
gettin' too busy to work. My job's been

interferin' with me a good deal lately. I'd give it up only for one thing."

" What's that ? "

" W'y, the dough, of course. You will have to smoke up, sure enough. Now I think I'll do a little work so as to get through early. Mame and me want to do a century by 4 o'clock. I went eighteen miles before breakfast this morning. I may be a sloppy rider, but I'm one of the best 150-pound liars in the business."

" Well, get to work," said Miller. " I'm going to be busy myself."

" What are you hurryin' to get through for? You ain't got nothin' in this world to live for. You're nothin' but a chair-warmer."

" Never you mind. Some day I'll fool you."

" Well, if it happens I'll be fooled all right, all right."

And with that he went to work.

IE'S MOTHER

XX

A full moon was hanging over the lake. The whole surface of small, uneasy waves was lighted. There was one path of shiny splendor leading straight out toward the moon and where this path lost itself no one could tell.

"There ain't no moon or nothin' to-night," observed Artie. He had been flipping pebbles down the paved beach and into the water. Mamie sat with him on the stone uplift dividing the park driveway from the slope toward the water — with him, to be sure, but three or four feet away, with her hat in her lap. "It's *perfectly* lovely to-night," she said.

The two bicycles were leaned over against the stone uplift and the lamps

ARTIE

threw oblong splotches of light on the gravel.

Behind Artie and Mamie was the gloomy range made by the heavy foliage of the park. In and out amid the dark banks of trees and along the level driveway moved glow specks like so many busy fireflies. Artie saw none of these, for he was intent on the spectacle of water and moonshine.

"The guy that could put all that into a picture'd be a bird, eh, Mame?"

"It's *perfectly* lovely."

"That's what it is, all right. They don't grow many like this one."

"I could stay out here all night and just look at the lake."

"Could you? Well, I think about two o'clock in the morning I'd be ready to let go. It *is* a peach of a night, though, I'll say that."

"Sing something, Artie."

"What do you want me to do — drive

184

the moon in? How did you ever come to think I was a singer? That's two or three times you've sprung that on me. Somebody must 'a' been stringin' you."

"Why, the night we walked home from Turner Hall you sang something awfully pretty. What was it?"

"Well, let it go at that. Any singin' I ever done was a horrible bluff, I'll tell you those."

"Oh, you contrary thing! You can sing if you try to."

"I take no chances, Mame. If I'd ever spring one o' them bum notes you'd gi' me the horse laugh and then there'd be trouble."

Mamie laughed and said: "What a boy you are! You never do anything I want you to."

"Come off! I'll tell you right now that when I kick on singin' I'm doin' you the greatest favor in the world. You never heard me sing. I guess you're a

185

ARTIE

little mixed in your dates. It must a'
been somebody else you had on your staff
that night."

" Why Artie Blanchard, you mean
thing ! "

" Hello ! Did I land on you that
time ? "

" I think it was awfully mean of you to
say that. I don't ever ask you if you've
been running around with some other girl."

" Why don't you ? I'd tell you there's
three or four others that kind o' like my
style."

" They must be hard up."

" Is that so ? Maybe I ain't so many
but I'm a purty good thing, at that. I'm
fresh every hour. No family ought to be
without me. When you lose me you lose
a puddin', and do n't you overlook it."

In answer, Mamie picked up some of
the small pebbles and threw them at him.
He held his cap over his face and laugh-
ingly begged of her to stop.

" Will you be good ? " she asked.

" Sure thing. But do n't be so rough with your man."

" My man! " Mamie tilted her head back, looked up at the moon and shrieked with laughter.

Artie was always vastly pleased to have Mamie understand his bantering way. He had often wondered if they would ever come to the habit of taking each other seriously. Could married people keep up the joke ?

" I seem to be makin' a horrible hit with you to-night," he remarked, as Mamie slowly recovered from the attack.

Mamie looked at him seriously for a moment and again broke into laughter.

" What's the joke ? " demanded Artie. "Put me next so I can get in on the laugh."

" Oh, nothing. Only you said that so funny."

" Funny? That was on the level."

At this moment Artie had an inspira-

tion. The conversation was headed.
right. Why not steer it straight ahead?

"Of course," he continued, "I was
kind o' kiddin' when I said that, but when
it comes right down to cases it was n't so
much of a kid after all."

Mamie laughed a little, but it was a
forced laugh. She had suddenly become
interested in a pebble which she was rolling
under the toe of her shoe.

"I do n't mean more 'n half I say,"
said Artie, tightening his fists with resolution and still looking out at the illumin-
ated lake, "but on the dead, Mame, I ain't
as foolish sometimes as I am others. That
talk about there bein' any other girl was
all guff."

"Pshaw, I knew that."

"Gee, you know you 've got me right,
do n't you? And I guess you have, too.
That ain't no lie. Say, Mame, what do
you think? Miller was roastin' me the
other day. He said I was slow."

" Slow — how ? "

" About doin' the nervy thing — comin' out and sayin' to you, ' Here, let 's fix it up.' "

" Fix what up ? "

" Oh, you do n 't know, do you ? You ain 't got no notion at all of what I 'm gettin' at, have you ? That 's too bad about you."

Mamie began to laugh and then she checked herself, for she observed that Artie was frowning.

" Of course," said she, " I suppose you mean — that we —— "

" All I mean is, what 's the matter of gettin' it settled that it 's goin' to be a case of marry ? "

There ! When he said this it seemed to him that his voice went further and further away from him, as if some one else were speaking the words.

Mamie was smiling quietly and turning her hat over and over.

ARTIE

" I guess that did n't scare you so much
after all, " said Artie, who at that moment felt that his whole existence had
stepped out from under a burden.

" No," she replied, as she continued to
fuss with the hat. " Scare me ? "

" How about it bein' up to you ? "

" Oh, it's all right, I guess." She
spoke with a frightened attempt to be
careless.

" This is one of them cases where all
guessin 's barred."

" Well, you might know it 's all right."

" It's a go then. "

He said this rather solemnly. There
was a pause, and then he continued with
some embarrassment: " I 'll tell you,
Mame, it seemed to me we ought to have
it through with. I did n't want to keep
you guessin' whether I wanted to stick.
Do n't you think it was the wise move—
huh ? "

" It 's all right — yes."

" I was goin' to spring it on you sooner, but I ain't never got the nerve to talk much about things like that. It ain't like askin' a girl to go to a show, is it?"

" Not exactly," and then both of them laughed, in a relieved way.

" Do n't you think you 'd better put your mother on to it?" asked Artie.

" I do n't know. Would you?"

" Sure. I guess she won't make no holler."

Mamie laughed again. " That's a good one on you," she said.

" What is?"

" She wanted to know the other day if you 'd asked me yet."

" Who, the old girl? Well, what do you think of that? Everybody's on to us, Mame."

" I do n't care."

" Care? They can bill the town with it if they want to. Come on; let 's take another whirl through the park."

PRINTED AT THE LAKESIDE PRESS
FOR HERBERT S. STONE & CO
PUBLISHERS, CHICAGO

A RTIE, a Story of the Streets and Town, by GEORGE ADE, with many pictures by John T. McCutcheon. 16mo, $1.25.

These sketches, reprinted from the *Chicago Record*, attracted great attention on their original appearance. They have been revised and rewritten and in their present form promise to make one of the most popular books of the fall.

THE FEARSOME ISLAND, being a Modern rendering of the narrative of one Silas Fordred, Master Mariner of Hythe, whose shipwreck and subsequent adventures are herein set forth. Also an appendix accounting in a rational manner for the seeming marvels that Silas Fordred encountered during his sojourn on the fearsome island of Don Diego Rodriguez.

By ALBERT KINROSS, with a cover designed by Frank Hazenplug. 16mo, $1.25.

IN BUNCOMBE COUNTY, By MARIA LOUISE POOL. 16mo, $1.25.

A series of sketches of Country Life in the South. They are much in the style of Miss Pool's "A Dike Shanty," which has been so successful.

To be had of all Booksellers, or will be sent postpaid on receipt of price by the Publishers.

HERBERT S. STONE & CO., CHICAGO.